Someone Is Killing the Great Chefs of Europe

Nan and Ivan Lyons

BALLANTINE BOOKS • NEW YORK

Library of Congress Catalog Card Number: 75-45140

ISBN 0-345-32368-8

This edition published by arrangement with Harcourt Brace Jovanovich

Manufactured in the United States of America

First Ballantine Books Edition: July 1985

eking duck. Lacquered to perfection. Crisp skin. Warm moist pancakes. Spring onions and sweet bean sauce. Yes. If he were to leave London immediately, within eighteen hours he could be in Peking.

The black Phantom VI Rolls-Royce spilled noiselessly down South Audley Street and into Grosvenor Square. Achille van Golk grunted as he lifted his leg onto the jump seat in front of him. The pain. He narrowed his eyes and blotted out the white gold of a ten o'clock sun. He envisioned himself at Fung Tse Yuan, nodding with approval as Chen awarded the glistening honeyed duck to him. Indeed, had he not traveled farther for it than Marco Polo?

Pushing her pram onto the zebra, a nearsighted nanny stepped off the curb. The Phantom VI caught its breath sharply. "What is wrong with him?" Achille shouted through the glass to his secretary in the front seat. "Is he trying to kill me?"

The new black chauffeur (Rudolph) turned his semi-Afro-sheared head quickly toward Miss Beauchamp (pronounced *Beechum*). "There is nothing wrong with him," she said, without turning around to her employer, "except that he is *not* trying to kill you."

"Where did you find him? Where is he from?"

"Poland," she answered.

Achille was silent. His leg throbbed and he was chilly. He hunched his shoulders and pressed the sable collar of his black vicuña coat against his ears. He opened the rosewood bar and stared in disbelief at the three empty crystal decanters and the empty silver bowl. He snatched the microphone from its perch.

"Miss Beauchamp" (pronouncing it *Beauchamp*), "would you be good enough to explain to me, in front of your friend Stanislaus, why my decanters are empty and most especially explain to me why my nut dish is not filled with my nuts?"

"You should not have them."

"I did not appoint you Keeper of the Cashews. Kindly remember you are a vastly overpaid boring spinster whose nonessential duties do not include sequestering my nuts or employing the Prince of Zanzibar."

"He is from Poland. Outside Cracow."

"Mozambique is outside Cracow."

"We're here," she said, turning around for the first time. She allowed a small smile. "Does your leg hurt?"

Rudolph slid out of his seat and came around to open the door for Achille. Raising the enormous arms of his black fur-lined overcoat, Achille held on to him. They rocked back and forth until momentum propelled the bald man with one black eyebrow across his forehead out of the car. Achille brushed away the hand that helped him and walked painfully toward No. 44.

Miss Beauchamp rang the bell, and stood well back to allow Achille to fit through the door with ease.

"Good morning," the nurse said, rising and pointing to the inner office, as though just having been chastised for not having risen quickly enough. "Dr. Darling is expecting you. Go right in."

Miss Beauchamp opened the second door and Achille snorted before crossing the threshold. Andrew Darling, M.D., stepped from behind his drawerless desk and thrust forward a well-manicured hand. "Achille, how good to see you up and around." He spoke in a voice one decibel below creating a public nuisance.

"Of all those people who have stuck their fingers up my ass, you are the last by whom I wish to be called Achille."

"I'm your doctor!"

"Your perverse choice of vocation does not endear you to me, however pleasurable *you* have found my previous examinations. Nor am I particularly charmed by your latest medical fetish. Here." Ach-

3

ille took a small bottle from his pocket and tossed it. Dr. Darling caught the specimen bottle with an audible intake of breath, and looked down to assure himself that the cap was tight. He saw written across the label in thick red marker *Mis en Bouteille au Château.*

Dr. Darling stepped back and placed the bottle on a corner of his desk blotter. "Do sit down, Mr. van Golk. I'm afraid I have some rather serious news for you."

"Peter Pan has stolen your children again."

"Please have a chair," Dr. Darling suggested, ignoring Achille's comment. "Are you certain you don't wish to be alone?" he asked, nodding politely at Miss Beauchamp.

"I am alone."

Miss Beauchamp glared at Achille. He shut his eyes for a moment and then sat down.

"Don't you wish to remove your overcoat?" the doctor asked.

"Is your diagnosis to take us through a change of season?"

"Mr. van Golk," he bellowed, "you are not a well man."

"Which is precisely why I came here rather than to my florist, however incorrect my instincts are beginning to prove. Doctor Da . . . , see here, I am a very busy man with a very busy schedule. And who knows what dermatological adventure you may have lurking around the corner. I suggest we save one another some time. How long do I have to live?"

"That will depend entirely upon you."

"It relieves me to know it does not depend upon you, darling doctor."

4

"Mr. van Golk, the results of our tests have already shown you to have gout, an enlarged liver, a duodenal ulcer, a spastic colon, severe hardening of the arteries, and a nasty case of the hives. You are calamitously obese. Unless you take immediate action to lose one-half your present weight, you will die of cardiac arrest within the year."

"Doctor, surely there is no need to beat about the bush."

"I regret I find no humor in your case, Mr. van Golk. Indeed, it is ironic that the publisher of LUCULLUS . . ."

"The publisher of LUCULLUS is the publisher of LUCULLUS precisely because he has eaten his way to the top. You will remember, darling doctor, I am not the publisher of *The Tuna Fish Gazette*. I have shaped the eating habits of millions so they might appreciate the most civilized of the arts, despite your medical hysterics over egg yolks. My body is a veritable canvas on which creative geniuses have developed their techniques. I am, myself, therefore, a living work of art. Every fold, every crease, every chin is the signature of creation. I am, doctor sweetheart, thrilled by the flowering of my own flesh."

"Mr. van Golk, I do understand the unusual nature of this case. It is indeed unfortunate that so renowned a gourmet as yourself is faced with this problem, but you simply have no alternative. Unless you stop eating," he said, lowering his voice for emphasis, "you will most certainly die. All this food will kill you."

Kill me? The thought angered Achille. Not if I kill it first.

"You must take immediate action."

I must take immediate action, Achille thought.

"You must attack the root of the problem."

The chefs, Achille thought. The chefs are the root of the problem.

"You must begin to diet," whispered Dr. Darling.

Indeed, I must. The Ultimate Diet.

LUCULLUS LTD

Staff Memo

From: Typing Pool (Loretta)
To: Miss Beauchamp

Dear Miss B:

I've completed transcribing Mr. van G's tapes of yesterday. I trust you will find my work has been satisfactory and in spite of a personal problem over which I have no control you will give me a satisfactory letter of reference. I have worked for this firm nearly two years and always gave "above and beyond" as one might say. My respect for Mr. van G was always of the highest and I may say I regard his action as highly unusual.

Since I shall no longer be affiliated with this firm, I should appreciate your returning the six shillings I contributed to Sheila's wedding present. I have attached to these memos my unused luncheon vouchers.

FROM: AVG
To: Skeffington, Art Dept

Your proposed cover for the Easter issue is wretched. I doubt it could stimulate a Biafran's appetite, although the salami addicts in your department obviously thought their photo of a plexiglass pig stuffed with apples the height of nouveau garde. It stinks. I want to see flesh. I want to see a cover that would make Lazarus rise. Else you can go back to designing anchovy tins at Fortnum's.

FROM: AVG
To: Worthington, Editorial Dept

What have you got against leeks? I have searched through the copy for the Easter issue and cannot find them in one dish. Was this some amnesiac oversight or would you have me believe that you knowingly deleted my favorite veg from our sacred Easter issue?
FROM: AVG
To: Bussingbill, Mail Room

Your suggestion that we re-create the menu from

The Last Supper in our forthcoming Easter issue is one of the most vulgar ideas I have ever received. If you wish to remain in my employ through Lent, keep your mind on delivering Her Majesty's Mail. With dispatch.

FROM: AVG
To: Aldingham, Senior Editor

What the hell did Jesus eat at The Last Supper? Worth a two-page spread?

To Her Royal Highness Queen Elizabeth

May it please Your Majesty,
A note of reassurance that I have organized a truly brilliant dinner next month to honor Mr. Westlake, the departing ambassador to Bolivia. I don't know what old Bunky ever did (short of introducing your uncle to Wallis Simpson) that could provoke your banishing him to spend his old age tarnishing in some wretched tin mine. No matter. Bunky will be feted as befits a departing fusilier, who may himself, within weeks, become an hors d'oeuvre for some Andean hammersmith. I believe this dinner to be the best I've organized for you—from the superb "Pigeonneaux en Croute" of the Savoy chef to the spun sugar dessert that will be prepared by Miss O'Brien, who is flying in from New York. (Fear not, the illegal booty of Richard the Lion-Hearted will not be tapped. The "en Croute" and the "Bombe Richelieu" are at my own expense because they are the first and last courses of my most favorite dinner.)

9

I anticipate the evening with the greatest pleasure. If you are searching for a way in which to express your appreciation for my efforts, consider Barbados.
Your obedient servant.

FROM: AVG
TO: Beauchamp

Call Holstma at Swissair. Inform him there was no Perrier on my flight last week. For a supposedly neutral country, they've produced the most inflammatory people I've encountered. In view of my recent dietary restrictions, I am to be seated in the first row. No one is to be seated beside me. No one is to ask whether I wish anything to eat. Simply, one of those cheesy Swiss misses is to have ready a well-chilled bottle of Perrier and a wine glass. Holstma is to inform his airline personnel of this regimen. Since I go to Geneva every Thursday, I do not wish to endure a weekly confessional over so noncaloric a beverage. If he gives you any trouble tell him I shall print an article claiming that fondue produces cancer.

Natasha O'Brien will be arriving for Bunky's dinner. She is to be my guest throughout her stay. Give her the suite at the Connaught, although she's probably still alley-catting it with Louis. Find out. I want to know everything. Every detail. Send her roses from me. And perhaps a little marzipan.

FROM: AVG
To: Dr. Enstein

I wish to report I am deeply concerned over a decline
in the condition of my wife. While I was at the clinic
last week, she hardly conversed with me at all and at
one point was nearly unable to distinguish between
the Rhine wine and the Moselle we tasted at lunch.
When I entrusted her to your care thirteen years ago I
expected she would at least maintain some contact
with reality. I must report I am sadly disturbed by her
lack of improvement and wish to remind you that flying to Geneva each week to sit beside a virtual zombie
is not one of the high points on my agenda.

In answer to your recent inquiry, your name has
been added to our complimentary subscription list.
Your first issue should reach you in about six weeks.

FROM: AVG
To: Beauchamp

I want Natasha picked up at Heathrow next month.
Send the red Rolls.

FROM: AVG
To: Louis Kohner

Sehr Gehert Herren,
OUR Natasha will arrive at the Palace in MY red
Rolls. So much for pumpkins.

Love and
kisses,
A.

P.S. I, too, will arrive at the Palace (but not through the Service Entrance) and will personally review the dinner for LUCULLUS. Better get the lead out of your pastry.

URGENT

To: Beauchamp

Loretta is to be given a month's severance and fired the moment you receive her transcripts. Ketchup has been found in her desk.

atasha O'Brien had been awake nearly twenty-four hours. Body time was 7:00 A.M. September ninth, despite her fickle Piaget insisting it was noon. Even her loose chestnut Kenneth-cut hair was at twelve o'clock high. Her pink Chanel suit was imperiously unwrinkled. Her face (her own) was clean, soap scrubbed except for a trace of silver Givenchy shadow around her very big brown eyes. She wore no lipstick. Ever. It was a question of taste.

She passed through British immigration, holding her maroon Gucci valise in one hand, and her red alligator Mark Cross case and her pink suede Hermès purse in the other. Walking under the track of green "nothing to declare" lights at customs she frowned at the agent as her alligator case hit against a low counter. It opened and twelve knives fell at his feet.

"Oh, fuck," Natasha said.

"Here, madam, I'll help you."

"Thank you so much." She took each knife as he handed it to her, ran her thumb across the blade to be certain there was no damage, and then carefully replaced each one in its proper slot. They rose together and he put his hand to her elbow.

"I wonder if we might have a word."

"These are not for resale. They're not even a gift," she said. "These are for personal use only." She smiled broadly at him. "You see, I have a job to do at Buckingham Palace."

His grip tightened on her arm and with his other hand he picked up her valise. "This way, madam. It won't take a moment."

"Double fuck." Natasha followed him into a small office. A picture of the Queen hung on the wall. Natasha raised one arm in a gesture of mock greeting. She slumped into the chair and handed him her passport.

"You were born in Vienna, Miss O'Brien?" asked the small gray man who flaunted a gray sweater under his gray jacket.

"Yes."

"Nice city, Vienna?" he asked, still without looking up from her passport. "I've never been there."

"Oh, you must go. You would love it. It's so gay and romantic. Why am I here?"

"But you're an American citizen?"

"Yes. You see, my father was an American who met my mother in Vienna during the war."

"I've never been to America either."

"Well, what can I say? It's even bigger than Vienna. You must go. You would love it. Would you mind telling me what this is all about?"

"Your mother was Austrian?"

"No. Actually, she came from yet another place you've probably never been. She was a Russian émigrée. Her parents fled from Russia before the Revolution and settled in Vienna."

"Russia, you say?" his voice rising perceptibly.

"Much too cold. You wouldn't like it. On the other hand, if you like the cold, it would be a terrific place for you. Especially if you like borscht. I would say, if you do like borscht, Russia is the place to be. May I go now?"

"Miss O'Brien," he said sharply, "why do you have all those knives with you?"

"I am a cook."

"I see." There was a pause as they looked at one another. "My wife," he continued slowly, "is a cook." Another pause. "She doesn't carry knives around with her."

"I am a professional cook. Actually, a rather famous, rich, beautiful American cook. I give classes, write articles and books, appear on television. . . ."

"Are you a chef?" he interrupted.

"That's it. That is it. You see, all chefs, all professional cooks, use their own knives. We take them from job to job like a doctor takes his own instruments. No good cook would ever dream of using anyone else's knives. It would be like asking Rostropovich to play on someone else's cello."

"He's Russian, too, isn't he?"

"Da."

"You were born in 1942?"

"Da."

He looked at her sternly. "Brown hair." He checked the passport for verification. "And brown eyes. Yes. Five feet four inches." He studied the photograph, nodded at her, and announced, "Well, this is certainly you."

"Goody."

"Tell me," he began slowly, "is it your intention, Miss O'Brien, while you are a visitor in Great Britain, to kill anyone with your knives? I mean to ask, do you plan on using them as lethal weapons?"

"Funny you should mean to ask."

He waited for her to continue. "Yes?"

"No. I'm afraid not. No matter how sorely tempted I might be, let us say, while having my privacy, integrity, and patience abused. Not even in those circumstances would I consider using my knives as lethal weapons." She shook her head. "Sad, but true."

"And you say you came all the way from New York to cook at Buckingham Palace?"

"At a dinner the Queen"—she pointed to the picture on the wall—"that Queen, is giving tonight."

"And the Palace actually asked you to come from New York?"

"I am actually being paid to do it."

"You were paid to come from New York to cook dinner at Buckingham Palace tonight," he said, careful to avoid making it a question.

"Not dinner. Just dessert. I'm here to make the dessert."

"You were paid to come from New York to make dessert at Buckingham Palace tonight?" he said, unable to control his voice from rising at the end of his sentence. "And that," he added, as if he were satisfactorily answering his own question, "is why you have a case full of knives."

"Thank God you understand." Then she added, smiling, *"Tovarich!"*

He picked up the telephone quickly and dialed two digits. "Please come in at once," he said and hung up immediately. He looked at Natasha and nodded, smiling as though he had seen her for the first time. He rose from his chair and said, "How do you do? I am Captain Henshaw, Airport Security."

Without rising, she extended her arm to shake his hand. "How nice to meet you, Captain. I am Natasha O'Brien, Airport Insecurity."

The door opened and a robust dark-haired woman in a blue uniform stepped inside. She closed the door smartly behind her.

"And this must be Mrs. Captain Henshaw, who helps you mind the airport."

"This is our Miss Creighton," he said. "She will . . ."

"She will not. Not one finger," Natasha said, rising from her chair. Miss Creighton narrowed her eyes and leaned forward like a bulldog eying a fly. "I will not have Our Miss Creighton lay a finger on me. Nor will I continue this absurd interview. I'm exhausted from my trip. Do you know how much work I've had to do in preparation for this trip? Do you know how many columns I've had to write? Even on the plane. With *coq au vin* yet. No. I am exhausted. If carrying knives is a crime, or if you think you've found Jacqueline the Ripper, then charge me formally. Call Scotland Yard. And get me a lawyer. Otherwise, open that door and let me go."

"Miss O'Brien, I'm merely trying to avoid making any formal charges or detain you any longer than absolutely necessary. I merely wish to examine your luggage, which we have every right to do, and our Miss Creighton will examine your person to be certain . . ."

"If you, and Our Miss Creighton, wish to be certain, Captain," Natasha said, pointing to the picture on the wall, "call the Queen."

Miss Creighton shot a glance at Henshaw and then narrowed her eyes again. How can Henshaw always spot the lunatics, she wondered.

"Miss O'Brien," he began.

"That Queen. Of England." Natasha turned to Miss Creighton. "C'mon," she said impatiently, "you must know the number."

Miss Creighton took one step forward, as though the pull on her lead had slackened for a moment. Bloody brilliant he is, she thought.

"Miss O'Brien, I would appreciate it if . . ."

"Captain, you will appreciate it if I do not charge you with kidnapping me. I am an American national detained against my will without sufficient cause. I am suffering a severe case of jet lag while on my way to serve Your Majesty, Her Majesty, Your Queen." Natasha opened her purse. Both Henshaw and Creighton pulled back instinctively and then relaxed as they saw her take out an envelope. She handed Henshaw the invitation. "So call. Someone must be home."

Silence. Like treacle. Then a throat-clearing from Henshaw. He folded the invitation neatly, placed it within her passport, and handed both to Miss Creighton, who, after receiving a nod from Henshaw, left the room to check Natasha's credentials.

Henshaw looked at Natasha, smiled quickly, and asked, "What is it you're making for dessert?"

"La Bombe Richelieu."

"Oh."

"It's made with chocolate ice cream, whipped cream, orange peel, almonds, raspberry ices, liqueur, and spun sugar."

"Indeed."

Pause.

"Yes."

Pause.

"Actually, Captain, you use over a dozen egg yolks."

"Over a dozen."

Pause.

"And tons of heavy cream."

"Sounds interesting."

"It's a specialty of mine. I created it."

"I see." Then, after a moment, "It doesn't sound overly complicated."

"It's not. Would you like the recipe for your wife?"

"It doesn't even sound as though there were very much . . . uh, cutting up of things."

"Not really. Once you've slivered the almonds and

19

peeled the oranges. Actually, it's become rather a bore for me to make. That's how easy it is."

"Then," he said, slowly rising from his chair, raising his voice with every word until he was shouting, "would you please tell me why the hell you had to be paid to come from New York with all your bloody knives to make a dessert that my wife could have made?"

The door opened. Miss Creighton entered briskly. She nodded affirmatively to Henshaw and handed Natasha her passport. Natasha smiled, and stood up to leave.

"Tell me, Miss O'Brien," Henshaw said, his voice hardly above a whisper, "do they do this sort of thing often at the Palace?"

Natasha picked up her luggage. "Only when they run out of Jell-O."

The ruby-red Rolls-Royce Silver Shadow sedan stopped at the Trade Gate of Buckingham Palace. A mustachioed, scarlet-coated officer glanced at the black chauffeur and walked immediately to the rear of the car. He bent over to look in at Natasha. She rolled down her window.

"Good day, Miss O'Brien. We've been expecting you. Hope you had a pleasant trip." Without waiting for a reply, he changed his tone. "Driver, please take the lady to the door immediately ahead and then return through this gate."

Rudolph glanced at her in the mirror. They raised their eyebrows simultaneously and prepared to share an adventure. A bellow from the officer. "You may open the gate."

"Yes, sir. Thank you, sir." Another toy soldier unlatched the gates and drew back first one side and then the other. The officer nodded to Rudolph that he might proceed.

De Mille himself could not have helped being impressed. The door was only some five hundred feet away, but crossing the gravel was to step through The Looking Glass. Each crunch of tire on stone crushed away reality. Ordinary objects that came into view—a door frame, a shrub, a fallen leaf—became subject to comparison with their counterparts in the real world. But it was mostly The Silence onto which everything else intruded. The car moving. The car stopping. Rudolph opening the door. The crunch of his steps as he walked around to open Natasha's door. She stepped out and held on to his arm for a moment. She looked at the Palace facade, staring as though she had never before seen its likeness. Pussycat, pussycat, where have you been?

Rudolph put her alligator case in front of the entrance. She smiled at him. There was nothing to be said, even if either of them had dared break the silence. He nodded and walked to the car. She heard the last of his steps as she turned to the door. PLEASE RING BELL.

An overly freckled, red-haired young man in blue-striped overalls appeared almost immediately. "Sorry to keep you waiting, miss. I'll take you to your room." He spoke with a soft Irish brogue.

"Thank you, but I'm here to cook. . . ."

"Yes, miss. *La Bombe Richelieu* it's to be."

The small foyer in which they stood was painted with cream-colored glossy enamel. The floors were tiled in black-and-white vinyl checkerboard squares. Above them, at overextended intervals, were large illuminated globes hung from the ceiling on heavy brass chains. The glow they produced had a very yellow cast, unlike American indoor lighting. Natasha felt as though she had checked into a resort on the Irish coast.

They walked down a hallway comprised of closed, numbered doors. A white-haired woman in a starched white dress with a starched blue apron and a starched blue cap came stiffly toward her.

"I am Mrs. Wooley," she said in a crashingly firm voice.

"And I'm *La Bombe Richelieu*," Natasha answered, smiling. The women shook hands. "I am pleased to meet you, Mrs. Wooley."

"You must be tired from your journey, Miss O'Brien. Simon will show you to a room where you may freshen up. When you're ready, please ring the bell and we'll take you downstairs."

Natasha followed Simon along another corridor of closed, numbered doors. No, it was more like checking into an orphanage.

"Here we are, miss." Simon stopped in front of No. 37. He took a large ring of keys from a hook on his belt and unlocked the door. The room was all glossy white enamel. The bed was framed by a white enamel headboard. A white enamel wooden chair sat next to a white enamel table. A vase of fresh red roses offered the only color in the room.

Simon turned on the light for her. Then he opened a closet to show her a white uniform, white apron, and white hat. "If these don't fit, miss, please ring and Mrs. Wooley will change them."

22

Natasha walked to the closet and handed the dress to Simon.

"Will you please ask Mrs. Wooley for a pair of trousers size twenty-four and jacket to match."

"But . . ."

"I can squeeze into a twenty-two."

"Thank you, miss." Simon closed the door behind him.

Natasha walked to the roses. There was a card. "You are the perfect ending to my favorite dinner. As always, A." She looked at her watch and subtracted five hours. Goddamn it, it was too early to think about *La Bombe Richelieu,* no less to begin separating eggs in some strange kitchen. She smiled. Some Strange Kitchen. Hell, she was going to play the Palace!

Mrs. Wooley was clearly displeased as they walked along the corridor on the lower level. The kitchens of Buckingham were unsuited to young women in trousers. Yet, it would have been unspeakably rude to insult the dessert.

"The Royal Family have their private suites in the North Wing," Mrs. Wooley announced, almost as much to reassure herself as to attempt civility with The American.

The corridors on the lower level had fluorescent lighting and the floors were tiled in a predominantly black multicolored marble pattern. The walls were the same glossy cream enamel. Men in blue-striped overalls were counting the crates of vegetables that lined the passageway. "Our vegetables are grown on the grounds of Windsor Castle and are picked fresh daily. Excesses are sold to tradesmen at Covent Garden." Natasha already knew this, having gone with Louis on his early-morning shopping. The Royal garden shipments were reserved generally for the deluxe hotels where the deluxe cooks were fanatic about freshly picked vegetables. Since it was not permitted to advertise the source of the produce, none of the other buyers at Covent Garden could capitalize on the lineage of their carrots.

As they passed boxes of flowers being unpacked, Mrs. Wooley continued her narration. "Flowers are grown also in the Royal sheds and are sent down daily. We even grow our own Christmas trees."

"Does Her Majesty . . ." Natasha began hesitantly.

"Yes?"

"Does Her Majesty really drink orange juice with every meal?"

"The door on your left leads to the Royal meat and game larders. The birds shot at Balmoral and Sandringham are kept in the basement refrigerators. There is also a large glass tank filled with fresh water and stocked with spotted trout from Loch Muick."

"I've also heard the salad is served as a first course."

"Mr. Cantrell, the Royal Chef, has asked that I extend to you every courtesy and suggested I show you the service hall before taking you to the kitchen."

"I mean, does she drink orange juice with things like pâté, or oysters?"

The corridor they turned into had a series of amber, red, and green lights along the walls. It was as though Natasha had just stepped onto a movie set. There were men carrying white satin knee breeches and scarlet frock coats. White silk stockings were being sorted in one of the rooms off the corridor, and some young men carrying blue vests with gold lace were being lectured to by a scarlet-nosed character out of Dickens.

"When the amber lights flash you will be in position for serving. Green lights will go on for commence of the service, as we have rehearsed. You are to stop dead in your tracks if the red light flashes. No one is to move if the red light flashes. Now that's all you have to remember. Look at the lights, gentlemen, and try to forget you are fugitives from a Wimpy Bar."

Natasha looked at Mrs. Wooley, who explained. "The Palace Steward stands behind Her Majesty in the dining room and is able to see the progress of the meal. At the appropriate time, he presses the buttons that alert the under-butlers, pages, and footmen for presentation or removal of each course. Since many of them are not permanent staff, the traffic lights were installed to ensure proper timing of the service. You have no idea how difficult it is to find experienced help. Everyone wants to be a film star these days."

Butterflies. In her stomach, the unbelievable reality of where she was. And the absurdity. In a few hours men in white stockings would be serving her dessert to the Queen of England. Eat your heart out, Betty Crocker.

Mrs. Wooley turned and led Natasha through a service area. "We'll be using the Queen's kitchen today. The Royal kitchens are reserved for state banquets." From the service area could be seen the preparations room, with its white tiled walls and long white tables running the length of the room. Kitchen workers in blue-striped overalls were cleaning vegetables and cutting joints of meat. There were the familiar sounds of steel against wood and the constant running of water.

In the working kitchen were stoves, electric ovens, and refrigerators in an unbroken line against the far wall. The equipment was a combination of modern and stone age. Blue cupboards lined the other walls and an open door showed shelf upon shelf of gleaming copper. Commanding one corner all for itself was an enormous juicer on a special table. To the right of the working kitchen was the pastry kitchen, in which Natasha would spend the next six hours.

The Royal Chef came out of his office. He was a very tall man with a very large nose and a very small mustache. "Miss O'Brien," he began with his Continental accent, "I am Phillipe Cantrell and I welcome you to our kitchens."

"Dare I proceed without a green light flashing?" she asked, walking toward him.

"Ah. Mrs. Wooley has given you the Cook's tour."

"Literally."

"Yes, a house joke. But you must be tired from your journey."

"And hungry. What are the chances for a Royal BLT down?"

He smiled. "You will forgive that I cannot myself prepare something for you, but I am sure Mrs. Wooley . . ."

"I'm only kidding. But I would love some coffee." She looked at the juicer in the corner. "And perhaps some orange juice, if you have any."

"If I have any?" Phillipe raised his hands. "You would not believe the juice A Certain Someone consumes." He lowered his voice. "With everything." Natasha smiled at Mrs. Wooley. Phillipe opened the book he carried under his arm and took out the list of ingredients Natasha had sent to him weeks ago. "We have everything ready for you. That is, if you do not mind that I did the buying for you?"

"Of course not. I trust you implicitly."

"Thank you. I will assign . . ." Phillipe was interrupted by shouting from the preparations kitchen. Natasha recognized the voice, and in a moment Louis rushed through the door, throwing mushrooms into the air. He wore a white uniform, and his toque hid a head of thick gray hair. A big man with craggy features, Louis looked younger and thinner than a few months ago, when Natasha had last seen him. She thought of how she loved the silver hair on his chest.

"You. Herr Royal Chef. You call these *champignons*? In thirty years I have not seen such an assortment of fungus. Do you expect me to cook them or cure them?" He had not noticed Natasha.

"Louis, they are Windsor mushrooms. The best in the Empire."

"Which is not to say much for the Empire. *Ach du lieber,* I should have done my own buying." Louis turned to Natasha, considering at first only the presence of another person to whom he could plead his case. Then recognition. *"Mon oignon,"* he drawled, opening his arms wide and embracing her as the mushrooms dropped to the floor.

Mrs. Wooley and Phillipe looked at one another with raised eyebrows. Oblivious to the chopping and simmering, sautéeing and fileting, Louis and Natasha began to rock from side to side. Silently embracing. She kissed his ear, bit it gently, and then whispered, "Poor darling, nobody knows the truffles you've seen."

Dear Sex Object:

I hope your baby blues fall out trying to read this note since it's being written under duress, under a hysterical "fasten seat belts" sign, and under the movie. If God meant woman to fly, She would have . . .

No matter, heartless wonder. I have once again surmounted all odds. Enclosed is "Sex and the Sommelier," the last column due you. It (like me) is too damn good for you. Or Sulzberger's yellow rag. It (the column) (my last) (I swear on your nonexistent agent's heart) (HEY—I just did three parentheses in a row!) (Are your toes curling, love?) (Six) I forgot what I was going to say. Oh. About the enclosed column.

AVISO—1) No cutesy subheads without my approval; 2) I have final say on all shots to be used—no matter how The Blue Fairy stamps his pointy little feet; 3) Better to cut your hairy wrists than to cut one line of my copy.

How sweet of you to send me a bon voyage bottle of NONVINTAGE champagne! Château Cheapeau has long been one of my very favorites. Haven't the months with me taught you ANYTHING?

The only thing I still owe you (literally, precious) is the script for the Good Morning Show. I don't know why they object to using film from the demonstration I'll be doing at Harrods next week. Hell, if my dessert is good enough for the Queen, it should be good enough for Miss Co-Host. Yes, I know. They want a "liberated lady something." Not that I ain't one of your leading LL's, but Fannie Farmer wasn't exactly a blot on the nation. (Don't tell Gloria.)

So what else is new? I'm glancing at my "month-at-a-glance" calendar and I've xxx'd out everything for the next two weeks, except for the aforementioned TV thing. (To be titled *A Quiche in the Dark*? Or *Moule over Miami*?) Caramba, I haven't had this much free time in years. And I'm going to have FUN, FUN, FUN.

Even if it kills me, kills me, kills me.

All right. So I'm sitting here, five miles above terra firma, and can't stop thinking earthbound thoughts. Somebody ought to do a paper about the effects of pressurized cabins on The Guilts. No wonder the astronauts turned to Tang.

In support then, of better mental health, here's the latest list of my priorities. Here's what I really want to do:

1. Set up that cooking school for kids. If the church can get them while they're young, why not me, too? (I know, because I'm not HER.)

2. Get on the Susskind show. I want to chew the fat with Jackie O's ex-liver-chopper, who says that if Escoffier lived today he would use margarine.

3. Get started on the eagerly awaited second edition of *You Are What You Eat,* my electrifying best seller. But this time, nobody but yours truly tests the recipes and the Yogurt Maven at your favorite publisher's had better keep her dentures shut. (Didn't you know she wore dentures? I heard she lost her teeth trying to eat the shells on her steamers.)

4. Paint my apartment. Laugh, but I cannot bear those white walls. I'm just not a vanilla personality. I'd never serve mashed potatoes and cauliflower on the same plate, so why should I have an all-white apartment? WHY? WHY? WHY? A lot you care.

5. Cancel my magazine column. But I know that I can't because you have to pay the seltzer man, and I should endure it with my other monthly curse. It's just that I don't believe anybody really cooks my recipes. Especially not when I've got a quarter page and Shake 'n Bake has three-quarters of

the same page. But who knows? Maybe
that's why people ride airplanes but also
buy flight insurance. I warn you, you'll
have a hassle trying to convince me to re-
new that contract.

Not just because I'm getting closer to London with
each air pocket, but I do keep thinking about Achille's offer. Mainly because as editor of LUCULLUS, I
could trust my audience. I know, I know, how could I
give IT ALL up and move to London? Maybe I can't.
Maybe it's just the Château Cheapeau talking. (I
had to drink it all myself because I was too ashamed
to offer it to any of my companions in first class—
which reminds me, they are definitely not all first-
class companions.)

Maybe I should give IT ALL up and get married?
Have kids? A shaggy dog? A station wagon? Or shall
I continue my life as a gastronomic Evel Knievel?
Jumping across flaming éclairs, leaping tall babkas
in a single bound?

No, I do not subscribe to your therapist Nor-
man's theory that these are the after-the-divorce
blues. I don't really think Max and I were ever
really married. Or at least, I wasn't ever really
married to him.

Anyway, just because I'm having a holiday is no
reason for you to sit back on your ten percent. I expect to come back and scream at you because there
won't be enough time to handle all the glamorous as-
signments you've snared for me. So much for What
Makes Natasha Run.

Do you think Paul Newman is really in love with
Robert Redford? They're right above me on the

screen. I can't hear what they're saying, but it looks kinda suspicious.

Speaking of sex symbols, I do miss you, puss. Not all of you, mind. Just the important part.

Kisses. All over it.
N.

he deep-blue Phantom Mark V Rolls-Royce turned the corner into Oxford Street. Maximilian Ogden lit an American cigarette. King-sized, filter-tipped, and mentholated. He inhaled deeply, and prematurely tapped the end of his cigarette into the ashtray.

"All right, Flanners. Let's knock off the Wimpy Bar on Wardour Street, and the Kentucky Pancake House near Leicester Square."

"Yes, sir," the chauffeur answered. "In that sequence?"

"Surprise me." Max sat back and brushed an ash from his camel's-hair coat. He was dressed in a gray

34

flannel suit with deep side vents in the jacket. His tie was pearl gray and he wore a gray-and-white-striped shirt with white collar and cuffs. He watched his reflection in the tinted window glass and thought he looked rather British. The graying temples, the large nose. Like Edward the something-or-other.

"You see, sir," Flanners began after an appropriate interval, "I'm afraid we're only around the corner from Wardour Street and in order to surprise you . . ."

"Around the corner?" Max asked without averting his eyes from the long-legged, miniskirted girl keeping pace with the car. "Now, that is a surprise, Flanners. You've done it again," he said, winking at his Oxford Circus appassionata.

"Well, yes, rather," muttered Flanners as he changed lanes and turned the corner.

These would be their last two stops. Mainly, to be certain they hadn't burned down the night before he mailed his report. And also because it was too early for his appointment with Achille.

Max's report to his board of directors at American Good Foods Products Enterprises was actually written on the flight over from Chicago, between the evening filet and the morning Rice Krispies. His analysis of quality-standards maintenance in a chain operation was lifted from a confidential study he had once made while moonlighting for the Israel Discount Bank when it was interested in underwriting a chain of kosher pizzerias.

His stopover in London was really unnecessary, because he already knew the precise spot he wanted for his first H. Dumpty omelette restaurant. But being there would give him a chance to see Natasha for the first time since their divorce became final.

"Wimpy Bar, sir. Surprise!"

Max looked out the window and stared into the half-empty premises. Some shopgirls on their way to a matinée, two Americans vying for the tomato-shaped ketchup dispenser, and a Jesus freak arguing with the turbaned Indian waiter. Typical. Probably they hadn't served a dozen burgers in the past two hours and the cook was either dozing in the men's room or else giggling over a year-old copy of *Playboy*.

"All right, Flanners. If you please."

"The usual, sir?"

"Yes. But this time with onion."

"Certainly, sir."

Flanners stepped out of the car, pulled on his gloves with a snap, angled his cap, and stepped into the Wimpy Bar. He walked directly to the turbaned waiter and repeated nearly the same order he had given at least twenty times earlier that day. Flanners had become a pro and didn't even glance nervously out at the car any more. He had accepted (somewhere around the fourth or fifth trip) that he and the American would be chasing hamburgers all day and threw himself, the matador from Maida Vale, into the sport. A few moments later he returned to the car.

"The cook was an earnest cockney, sir. The grill was reasonably clean, although the mustard and ketchup containers were rather grimy. The waiter short-changed me and never asked whether the salt or pepper was required."

"Flanners, you're brilliant," Max said, gingerly taking the bag from him through the open window.

"You've all the makings of a first-rate industrialist."

"Kind of you to say, sir. It's been rather an adventure."

"Well, I guess it beats waiting for fat ladies at Fortnum's. Now let's examine the damage."

Max pulled down the teak desk in front of him. He reached into the bag and took out a hamburger wrapped in a grease-stained paper napkin. He opened the napkin and noted the hamburger bun had been cut with a dull knife that pulled mercilessly at its top half. He took the top half off, careful not to soil his hands on the meat. The hamburger was depressingly flat, except for its concave center filled with grease. Holding the bottom of the bun, he flipped the hamburger onto the napkin. The slice of onion was cut evenly enough, but its outer rings were slightly shriveled from being left uncovered on a plate in the kitchen. Indeed, the entire onion, although spotted with rapidly coagulating grease and meat juice, was so dry that its inner rings had begun to separate. The thin membrane that held the petals together had dried completely. Testing the onion was a shrewd touch, he thought. Pity the report had already been written.

The inside bottom of the bun showed a smudge of dirt or rust, either from the cutting knife or from the underside of the metal turner. On the outside bottom of the bun, he saw telltale white spots that identified a careless baker who had not mixed his flour well enough. He reassembled the hamburger, careful to handle it as little as possible, put it back into the bag, and handed it to Flanners.

"For your collection."

"Thank you, sir." Flanners had neatly arranged some twenty bags on the floor in the front. Although he hadn't been instructed to do so, he had written on each bag the time and location of the purchase. If a job is worth doing . . .

Max rolled down the window and took a small can of nonscented deodorant from the cabinet above the desk. He sprayed the air, and used a damp cloth to refresh his hands. No unsung genius in that hamburger kitchen.

Flanners stopped in front of the brightly neoned Kentucky Pancake House. Max motioned that he needn't get out.

"Just looking, Flanners." Two cooks stood in a window where the grills had been placed so that passers-by could witness the birth of each pancake. For some bizarre reason, the cooks had pressed down their tall white hats into semiberet style. Their toques touched their ears and cheeks, and were totally flat on top. It angered Millie that some dumb manager hadn't understood that height was needed to circulate the air. He wasn't annoyed with the cooks, because he didn't expect they would understand anything.

"You ever eat here, Flanners?"

"Never," he replied, as though Commander Whitehead had just inquired about Pepsi-Cola.

"Good show," Max said, smiling at him. "And now on to Curzon Street, please."

No. 85 Curzon Street was a remodeled town house with bright-red shutters. An oval brass plate in finest Edwardian script identified the premises. LUCULLUS, it said, without saying nearly enough.

38

Max opened the bright-red door and was greeted by a blast of cold air. He smiled as he recalled Achille's comment that the Colosseum was the only properly ventilated structure in Europe.

A brisk "Good morning" came across the Regency table that served as a reception desk. The striking blonde smiled at him rather too professionally.

"You're new," Max told her.

"Miss Benson is on leave," she answered, unsettled by his familiarity.

"She's not pregnant again?"

The girl with the banana-colored hair smiled. Miss Benson was in her sixties. "May I help you?"

"Could be." Max sat down on the table, which had only a blank pad and a pink-feathered ball-point pen. "But first I have to see Mr. Wonderful. Tell the boss Millie Ogden is here."

"Millie?"

"Short for Mildred."

She picked up the phone, staring at him, and dialed. "Mr. Mildred Ogden to see Mr. van Golk. Yes, *Mildred*. Well, that's what he said. . . ."

Her eyes narrowed menacingly as she told him he might go upstairs. Max thanked her, smiled, blew a kiss, and walked into the small gold brocade elevator.

"Mildred, indeed," Miss Beauchamp said, opening the elevator doors. "But I am pleased to see you, Mr. Ogden. And not only because you're sure to upset His Nibs."

"From you that's a real compliment. Have you begun to lust after me, Beauchamp?"

"The way I lust after the plague," she snapped. They turned the book-lined corridor and faced the

39

etched-glass-and-copper swinging door that Achille had brought from a restaurant kitchen in Cannes. "I should tell you," she said, nodding at the gleaming door, "he's not been too well. I was hoping you might be rather discreet about it."

"How is Estella?"

"Mrs. van Golk, from what I gather, is in a decline."

Max looked at her, sensing the sincere concern she felt. He stared for a moment. "Tell me," he said softly, looking her squarely in the eyes, "have your breasts grown larger? They seem to be a different shape from . . ."

She closed her eyes in resignation, pointed to the door, and turned away. Max smiled, remembering how Natasha had kicked him in the shins for that remark. He pushed open the door and found Achille lying flat on his back atop a maroon leather chaise.

The office walls were covered with panels of brushed chrome with large brass nailheads. The floor was carpeted in red broadloom over which was centered a multicolored oriental rug. Red velvet drapes framed the floor-to-ceiling windows. The furniture was Regency. The vases and lamps and wall hangings were Chinese. One entire wall was covered with framed photographs of Achille eating in various restaurants. Each picture was autographed by the chef.

"Ah, the cupcake king," Achille muttered without opening his eyes. "Tell me, how many rat hairs are you now permitted to include in each frozen waffle?"

"I'm here because I ran short of rat hairs. Achille, you're looking dreadful."

"I have been given five minutes to live, having

consumed an immature Lafite at lunch. Good of you to share my final breaths with me."

"You know, Achille, if I didn't know you better . . ."

"Yes?"

"I would probably love you. You did get my letter?"

"Yes."

"Good."

"But I didn't read it."

"Achille. Can you be of help to me?" His voice was impatient.

"Of course I can be of help to you. You needn't have left your tin can to find that out. Indeed, who was responsible for your rise as one of the finest maîtres in Europe? Didn't I guide your career as though you were my own son? From Marseilles to Zurich to Vienna to . . ."

"Achille . . ."

"It was my hope we would someday open a restaurant that would surpass anything Europe has ever seen. Instead, you've become more corrupt than seedless grapes."

"American Good Foods is . . ."

"American Good Foods is a purveyor of cyclamates, nitrates, and saccharin. How many smiling American children have you poisoned this week?"

"Achille, I'm sorry if you can't understand that I like my work. I really do like flip-top boxes, and stay-seals, and frozen foods, and instant mixes. They are highly creative. And fun. And, unlike any restaurant kitchen, clean."

"And cleanliness is next to profits. That's the American way of life, isn't it?"

"Will you help me?"

"You do know that Natasha is here?"

"Here?"

"In London."

"I know."

"She's sleeping with Louis."

"Terrific."

"I thought you would want to know. I thought it my duty to tell you. Now, you see, I have been of help to you."

"Achille, I need a cook."

"For your H. Dumpty omelette brothels? Never."

"Don't you understand that one good cook at a place like H. Dumpty can improve things for thousands? Why is it that you people think you're running an exclusive club?"

"Kindly refrain from referring to me as a crowd."

"You know what I mean. You and Natasha sneer at the poor slobs who live on hot dogs but you won't give them a chance for something better. Help me hire someone really good. Give the poor slobs a fighting chance."

"How does *The Seven Apostles Delicatessen* sound? You know, Max, you're too old for this. And I have my hands full keeping 'the club,' as you put it, on its toes. Why, you should have tasted the *Bordelaise* they tried palming off at Montebello's. Dear boy, don't ask a *crêpe* to become a flapjack."

A pause. Both men unmoving. Then slowly, almost majestically, Achille put his legs over the edge of the chair and raised himself. He stood up and looked at Max for the first time.

"I still love you, dear boy. But I can't contribute to your ptomaine temple. It appalls me. Like glass sky-scrapers and one-size-fits-all. It's an inhuman, synthetic endeavor."

Max smiled. "You're a dying breed, Achille."

"Yes, I know," he said. And then, smiling broadly, "But do call me for lunch before you go to Paris. I've found a place that serves frozen turbot and canned peas."

The two men shook hands. They held on to each other for a long moment. "How is Estella?" Max asked. Achille withdrew his hand and shook his head. Max turned and closed the door behind him. No sooner had he taken two steps than Miss Beauchamp approached him.

"No whiplashes visible."

"You know," he said, ringing for the elevator, "you've really got TNT."

"And just what does that mean?" she asked warily.

"Two Nifty Tits."

CONFIDENTIAL

Hiram Baby,

As I said on the Don Ameche, get your arse on a plane and walk to the corner of Piccadilly and Haymarket. Throw your eyes two shops down and just look at that army surplus store. Eggs-actly what we want!

Since the three most important factors in a successful restaurant of this type are location, location, and location (in that order), you'll find that I'm not eggs-aggerating in my enthusiasm for this spot. Yes, I got the option, for only one month though, so we must get our eggs-perts on it pronto.

O.K. I'll stop eggs-asperating you. But you must admit there's a certain charm to my boyish enthusiasm. Indeed, I even bowled over old Achille. For all his sophistication, he was quite taken with H. Dumpty and suggested we might even want to open in Chelsea at the same time. Even better, he suggested that Louis Kohner (a cook I've known for some years) might be ready for a change and if we can make the price high enough, we might be able to catch ourselves a really big fish. (I told you it would be a good idea to stop off in London.) Kohner was in the Austrian army during WWII and was assigned to the kitchen. Well, the poor schnook learned a trade in spite of himself and potted around Vienna (Ha Ha) after the war before landing a job at Demel's (translation: the world's most fattening tearoom, with a very justified reputation for the best pastry anywhere). Louis married, but had no kids. His wife was also a cook and they decided to take a job in Brussels. From there to Brighton, and then the Savoy in London. How's that for some nifty PR? SAVOY CHEF TO DIRECT NEW OMELETTERIA CHAIN. The only problem is that there was some personal trouble when he and his wife split up (she's still in Brighton) and he's a little meshuga over the whole thing.

The upsetting thing is that Achille is rather busy and couldn't spend as much time with me as he had wanted. I've decided therefore to hang around for another day before heading for Paris. I don't want there to be any loose ends in London. (God, how I hate traveling around like this.)

About Paris. If for some reason I can't nail Louis— and I'll even stay another day to try to—I have no doubt that we can do well with any one of half a dozen French cooks I know who would sauté their mothers if it meant more money.

Tell Brian OEUF-OEUF is too cutesy for the Paris operation. Is he certain that Humpty Dumpty is not in any French nursery-rhyme books? Tell him also to check in Italian because NUOVO UOVO is just as bad.

Now about the enclosed report. It's brilliant. You don't even have to read it. Just make copies and circulate it. You'll probably get some flack from BIG WHITE CHEF, but I do insist that eggs not be opened until the moment they're to be used. The cooks will have to make this concession, although they prefer having everything premixed. Since we're just using fresh eggs, there's no reason to have a mix standing around getting tired and dirty when nature has provided us with the perfect "crack pack." Aside from this, I don't think there should be any problem. The whole thing is so goddamn right, it can't miss.

O.K. I'll be at the Plaza in Paris. You can reach me there. I'm off now for a little well-earned R&R. The pigeons in Trafalgar Square await!
Max

HAND DELIVER TO CONNAUGHT HOTEL—MS. NATASHA O'BRIEN

Nat—

For old times' sake? I won't leave my room till I hear from you. I miss you, babe. Even though.

Millie

Natasha and Louis lay together in his bed. Naked and asleep.

Louis Kohner's flat was a one-room studio near Cheyne Place on the embankment opposite Battersea Park. After his separation from Hildegarde, Louis sought the Battersea area because it reminded him of Brighton. From his windows he could see the reflection of the amusement-park lights, and even hear an occasional strain from the carrousel. Brighton had been a happy place. There had been good cooking and good loving.

Three floor-to-ceiling windows covered one end of Louis' rectangular studio. In front of the windows, as a painter would position his easel, Louis had commissioned a huge circular cooking area—sink, stove, oven, refrigerator, and generous work space. Above the circular butcher-block work surface was a round brass-and-copper pot rack from which hung a complete catalog of pots and pans. To one side of the island was a small alcove lined with over a hundred huge cork-topped test tubes filled with spices of every color and texture. The opposite alcove was filled with cookbooks, piles of newspaper clippings, menus, and notebooks.

The other walls were hung with prints and original oil paintings, all still lifes—fruit, game, vegetables, fish. A well-worn rectangular table with eight armchairs stood in front of the cooking area. The only other furniture in the room was a gleaming ornate brass bed that was angled in a corner.

It was morning. Louis had sensed it even without opening his eyes. "Tasha," he murmured to reassure himself. He turned to lie on his stomach, careful to position himself so that his genitals rested on the open palm of her outstretched hand. He opened his eyes to find her mouth, and as they kissed, her fingers involuntarily tightened around the stiffening pressure on her palm. They kissed again, their eyes open.

"I do so love to be wakened by a cock growing," she said.

"You're hurting," he said, pulling back slightly, as she released her grip.

"I'm sorry, *Liebchen.*" She raised herself and bent forward to kiss his penis. Then she stretched out, her head resting on his leg as she began to lick and caress the wounded area. Louis arched his back and

48

moved his head so that he pressed his nose between her legs. She felt his tongue start to search inside her.

"You know," she said as she began licking the length of his penis, "you could stand a little salt, darling."

Louis raised his head, breathing hard. He used the back of his hand to wipe the moisture from his lips. "Had the recipe been mine, I would have added tarragon."

"Don't be ridiculous, love," she said, catching her breath as she took the head of his penis from her mouth, "you never knew the right use for tarragon." She cupped her hands around his testicles. "For example, that salad in Rouen . . ."

Louis narrowed his eyes while his fingers continued exploring deep inside her. "And what was wrong with my salad in Rouen?"

"Oh," she moaned in response to the strength in his hand. "I told you, love, it was the tarragon that was all wrong."

"It was a superb . . ." He winced sharply. "Don't bite," he said. "It was a superb salad."

"No, darling," she answered, breathing heavily, "I'm sorry, but I didn't mean to bite that hard. The salad was a disaster. You just can't add tarragon to endive without making the endive schizophrenic. Oh, that's marvelous," she whispered.

Louis was on top of her. Her arms closed tightly around him. He began to penetrate. Slowly, slowly, slowly as he asked her, "And what did you think of my *Pigeonneaux* last night?"

Natasha pressed her fingers into his back. "*Ach,*

mein Führer, the only thing better than your cooking is your fucking."

Louis was taking a shower, and Natasha sat up in bed with the sheet pulled around her waist. If only they loved one another, she thought. Really loved one another. With passion and need, rather than affection and guilt. It was Louis who had taken her in as a child after her mother died. In truth, Louis and Hildegarde. They fed and clothed her, taught her a trade, got her a job as apprentice at Demel's. Natasha had never known her own father, and Louis was "Papa Louis" to her, at least until her late teens, when she and Papa Louis would make love while Hildegarde was in the shop baking *Schwarzwälder Kirschtorten.*

Perhaps the problem was they had already known each other too well and cared for each other too much when they first became lovers. They were never emotionally insecure together, never sexual competitors. They were one, closer than she had ever been with Max. But she had felt more of a woman with Max.

Louis opened the door to the bathroom and a cloud of steam escaped, announcing his entrance. He was naked, still dripping from the shower and drying himself with a towel. "So, now that you are divorced, why did you ever marry him?"

"I don't know. He detested oral sex."

"I never liked him."

"Who would you have liked for me, Papa Louis?"

"Don't call me that." He turned and walked into the bathroom.

"Hey, Louis," she called.

"Yes?"

"You still got the world's cutest ass."

She remained in bed while he dressed. It was 6:00 A.M. and Louis was already late for his morning marketing at Covent Garden. She remembered the first time she had gone there with him, horrified at seeing the transition from lover to Gestapo agent. ("Where are you hiding the good eggs? Don't lie to me about these raspberries, I am not a fool. You will get me the flour I require. Would you wish to see your relatives eat these carrots?") The second time, she followed behind him, listening and watching as he made unyielding demands upon the tradesmen. He sometimes spent half an hour selecting onions. Often he changed his day's menu if the carrots were not good enough for the garni, if the veal was not pink enough for the pâté. Natasha would remain, at a safe distance, in embarrassment and in awe. But she always went, following behind him because it was at the market that she really learned to be a cook.

"Who's in the kitchen at Arnaud's?" she asked.

"Tuesday? Marco is off. It must be Mercurio."

"Ugh. Is Franco still at Le Gigot?"

"No. He was fired for spitting in the soup. He went back to Lyons. They have some Greek refugee now who puts feta cheese in his *Béarnaise*.'

"Well then where shall we eat?"

"I am thinking," he said, putting on his coat. "Chinese is the least aggravating. Lee is still on Frith Street."

"I'll see you there at eight."

He walked to the door. "What will you do all day?"

"I have to see Achille later."

"That pig. Do you go to bed with him?"

"Why, Louis." She smiled teasingly. "That would be like sleeping with my father." He slammed the door.

It was after seven when Natasha walked into the lobby of the Connaught. She had her room key and went right upstairs without stopping at the desk.

At eleven she was awakened by someone knocking on the door. "What is it?" she asked, putting on her robe. "I hope for your sake it's a fire."

The knocking continued and she opened the door.

"Good day, miss. Are you Natasha O'Brien?" A tall, pinkish, balding man with steel-rimmed glasses looked at her.

"What do you want?"

"Are you Miss O'Brien?"

"Yes, I are. Who are you?"

"I am Detective Inspector Carmody of New Scotland Yard."

"Oh, not about that business at the airport . . ."

"May I come in?"

"Why? What do you want?"

"Do you know Louis Kohner?"

"Yes. Why? Has something happened?"

"May I come in?"

"What is it? What's happened?"

Detective Inspector Carmody walked past Natasha into her room. She closed the door and followed him.

"When was the last time you saw Mr. Kohner?"

"What the hell is it? Was he in a fight at the market?"

"Mr. Kohner is dead."

"Oh, my God. No." She sat on the bed. "There must be a mistake."

"I'm sorry."

"What . . . what happened?"

"I'm afraid he was murdered, miss."

"Murdered?"

"I'm sorry."

"Is this a joke? Did Max Ogden send you here?"

"Louis Kohner is dead."

"Murdered?"

"Yes."

"By whom?"

"We don't know."

She began crying. "But I just saw him. We . . . how?"

Detective Inspector Carmody cleared his throat. He looked directly into Natasha's eyes. "He was baked."

PIGEONNEAUX EN CROÛTE

4 pigeons serve 12
Only to be made in autumn

1. Wood pigeons from E. Nevins, 42B Covent Garden. In emergency, can use passenger pigeons from Mrs. Fortesque.
2. Rabbit—Harley's farm in Surrey. Also bacon (tell him "special fed").
3. Fresh truffles—Mr. Mimms. (Not big)
4. *Pâté ordinaire*—make dough 12-18 hours ahead
5. *Espagnole demi-glace* (arrowroot not potato flour)
6. Game aspic (tarragon vinegar)

Forcemeat:
  livers—quail, partridge, pheasant, hare,
    roebuck. choose 3. 250 grams mixed.
  pork belly 125 grams
  rabbit 250 grams
  foie gras 50 grams (add cognac and pistachios if "tinny")
  butter 25 grams
  egg yolks 3 (4, if small)
  espagnole
  mushroom peelings 75 grams
  chopped shallots 40 grams
  salt 20 grams

pepper 5 grams
cloves 2 grams
thyme sprig
bayleaf half
Madeira

1. grind forcemeat. add truffle ends.
2. bone pigeons.
3. stuff pigeons with forcemeat.
4. wrap each pigeon in bacon. sit one hour.
5. roll rectangular pieces of dough.
6. layer on dough: bacon, forcemeat, truffle. arrange pigeons. cover pigeons with layers of forcemeat, bacon, dough. shape rectangular.
7. seal edges. bake upside down. moderate heat.
8. cool. pour in game aspic jelly. sit one hour.
9. cut away crust on sides. shape.
10. turn over. cover top with chopped aspic. garni sides (cress).

As a first course, serve with champagne. Otherwise, a Romanée.

did not kill him, *Dummkopf.*"

Detective Inspector Carmody rose from his chair. He pulled a tissue from the box on his desk and handed it to the sobbing woman sitting opposite him. She took the tissue and threw it angrily to the floor. She opened her purse and put a scarlet handkerchief to her eyes.

"For real tears, a real *Taschentuch.*"

Hildegarde Kohner had been contacted at eight that morning by Detective Inspector Carmody. She was deep into braiding the dough for the luncheon rolls when Miss Penreddy, manager of the Bit O'Bavaria Tearoom, called her to the phone. On hearing that Louis was dead, she began crying hysterically until Inspector Carmody told her Louis had been murdered. She stopped crying at once and said he deserved to be killed and that *Gerechtigkeit* had been served. Carmody arranged for a young officer to accompany Hildegarde on the train from Brighton to London. Before leaving, however, Hildegarde put her rolls in the oven, and assured Miss Penreddy that Frau Muller, Hildegarde's landlady, would supervise the *Pinkelwurst mit Kartoffeln* planned for lunch.

Hildegarde walked with Young Officer Doyle to the railway station, and sat silently beside him on the trip to London while she vigorously sewed a black armband onto the sleeve of her suit jacket. She refused to ride in the police car that was waiting for them at Victoria Station. "I am not a *Verbrecher*," she said. "I will not ride in that. I will take the bus." Young Officer Doyle convinced her that the police car was there as a courtesy and not because she was considered a criminal.

Hildegarde was a small woman, under five feet, and still proud of her figure because it offered a public display of her private discipline. Her very orange hair, as intricately braided as her luncheon rolls, was piled high atop her head. She used herbal pastes on her skin and drank herbal teas but never used cosmetics, depilatories, or deodorants. Her body pleased her, not because it pleased others, but because it pleased her that she was healthy and clean and did not look as though she were fifty-eight.

"Certainly, Mrs. Kohner, I did not mean to imply that you are a suspect in the death of your husband." Hildegarde blew her nose. She used a tissue. "I real-

ize, Mrs. Kohner, how difficult all this is for you. And
I hope you realize that I'm merely doing my job."

"You are doing your job, because you like your job.
You, like all *Polizei,* enjoy death and crying and
making people feel afraid."

"Mrs. Kohner . . ."

"How did he die?"

Inspector Carmody cleared his throat and picked
up a piece of paper from his desk. It gave him a place
to put his eyes. "The coroner's report shows that the
deceased was struck on the back of the head and
knocked unconscious. Then his body was put into an
oven and incinerated."

"You mean," she began loudly, and then began
laughing uncontrollably, "that someone baked him?
Oh, no. That is not possible. Oh, God forgive me."
She stopped laughing. "That is not funny."

"The body was found at seven-thirty this morning
when a Mr. Sacristedes . . ."

"Frank?"

"You know him?"

"Of course I know him. He was Louis' *rechte Hand.*
Poor Frank."

"He's under sedation at Sister Mercy Hospital."

"Frank knew from the smell?"

"He knew something was wrong from the smell.
Of course, we've closed the Savoy kitchen until further notice."

"Oh, my God," she said, for the first time in genuine horror, "you've closed the Savoy kitchen?"

"At the insistence of the Health Service. It appears there are rather strict regulations . . ."

"So what will they do? Did they close the Grill as
well as the embankment side?"

"I don't know for certain."

"So what will they do? They could use the stoves for cooking, at least?" she asked belligerently.

"Mrs. Kohner, we are searching the kitchen for clues as to who might have done such a thing to your husband."

"But it's perfectly clear who killed him."

"Who?"

"Someone who hated him. A thief would kill him with a gun or a knife. No, Inspector, this murder is a special one."

"I agree, Mrs. Kohner. But who had a motive?"

She looked at Inspector Carmody. "First, I would check Albert Grives, 45 Kensington Gardens; he was Louis' assistant at the Savoy and I never liked him. I told Louis that Albert would one day kill him to get his job. Then, Seresh Jamba. He lives in Golders Green. Louis fired him to give the job to Albert. Seresh could never get work again and became an alcoholic. He made friends with a bartender and they opened a restaurant called Hurry Curry but it burned down the night it opened. And Jackson, Campbell, Hatney . . . all the fruiterers at Covent Garden. They would have killed him without a second thought. You must check a waiter named Harry Snape, who works in Brighton at the Farthing and Pence. He was the maître at Le Poulet Rouge when Louis was there. Harry was caught stealing truffles and vowed he would kill Louis. I don't know where Adamawitz is working, Lester Adamawitz. He lives in Surrey, with his sister who is crazy. Lester borrowed some money from Louis to have his gall bladder removed, he said. But he only wanted to buy a cart for the Rugby games on Sunday, where he could sell sandwiches he made on Saturday night using the food from the restaurant. Louis and I had a fight late one Saturday night, so Louis went back to the restaurant to roll some dough and found Lester stealing the supplies. Then you should find Rita Macedonia, who was a hostess at the casino in Brighton. She wanted Louis to sleep with her. But my Louis would never. This Rita Macedonia had already been in prison, I heard, for cutting the fingers off her lover. Rollo Ungt was the manager of Le Poisson d'Or in Kent, and Louis went to work there after leaving Brighton. Louis tried, but it was impossible. Ungt wanted only to serve fish that was frozen. Louis told him unless he put a tank in the kitchen to keep fresh fish, he would quit. Ungt promised that he would. Then he went to Woolworth's and bought a goldfish in a bowl and gave it to Louis. Louis served the goldfish to Mrs. Ungt for lunch. She had a heart attack and died in the dining room. Then there was Casimir Fenouiel. He was a writer of cookbooks who stole one of Louis' recipes. He published it as his own. Everyone knew it was Louis' dish, and whenever Casimir went to a restaurant, the chefs refused to cook for him. For almost a year, this Casimir thief would have to put on a disguise every time he went into a restaurant. Then, there is . . ."

"Mrs. Kohner, calm yourself, surely there are not more people who would have wanted to kill your husband?"

"Of course there were. Probably hundreds. He was a very popular man."

"But what I mean is, who do you think was actually capable of killing him?"

"Everyone was capable of killing him. It seems to

me that the question, Herr Inspector, is who stood to gain the most from his death."

"And who do you think would gain the most from his death?"

"How should I know that? I am the *Witwe* not the *Detektiv.*" Detective Inspector Carmody watched a small sneer part her lips.

"I was wondering, Mrs. Kohner, if we might not discuss further your late husband's . . . uh"—he stammered for a moment trying to find the right word—"your husband's relationship with Miss O'Brien. I mean to ask, what were your feelings about this relationship?"

"You mean to ask questions that will make you feel superior."

"Were you aware that your husband was having an . . . a relationship with Miss O'Brien?"

"Perhaps you are not secure as a man. Perhaps that is the reason you torture old women."

"Mrs. Kohner!"

"What do you think, *Wunderkind*? What do you think I felt about my husband sleeping with Tasha? He comes home one day with her, like you bring home a lost dog. I had no children. She was ten, eleven, twelve. I had no pets. So we kept her. No one else wanted her. I made her clothes. I fed her. *Nein,* more than feeding her, I was the one who taught her how to cook. She was my friend, my sister, my daughter. No mother could love a child more than I loved her. Does she know about Louis?"

"Yes. She was here this morning to make a statement."

"Did she tell you where she was last night?"

Carmody hesitated.

"Do you know she was making dinner for your Queen?" Hildegarde smiled. "I didn't do such a bad job, *ja?*"

"You must be very proud of her."

"I do not want to see her. I have not seen her in ten years."

"Then you knew about their . . . relationship?"

"I knew because Louis told me."

"He told you!"

"Yes. It was the morning after their first time together. He and I were alone. Rolling the strudel dough. I looked at him and I knew. I picked up the pastry scissors and put them to his neck. 'Are you sleeping with her?' I asked, pushing the scissors into his neck. '*Ja,*' he says to me." She began to cry. "You have never met such an honest man."

"Did Miss O'Brien know that you knew?"

"Not for a long time. What kind of person do you think I am? You have no feelings. Do you think I would tell her? And ruin her first affair? I told you I loved her. How wonderful for her to find someone like Louis. What more could any mother ask?"

Inspector Carmody stared at Hildegarde, uncertain how to proceed with his questioning. "Mrs. Kohner, would you mind telling me why you and your late husband separated?"

"Because we had been together for too long."

"I'm afraid I don't understand."

"You don't understand how two people can be together too long? *Mein Gott!* You British are so passionless you cannot understand lack of passion. Louis . . ." She hesitated. "*Ach, mein Schätze.*" She began to cry. And then after a moment, "My Louis was not an easy man to love. Even Natasha did not have an easy time with him. What do you think made her marry that American hot dog?"

"Do you think Mr. Ogden might have . . . ?"

"And dirty his lily-white hands? Ha! I tell you, *mein Kapitän,* I think he would have loved to kill Louis, but he would not have the courage."

"And Mr. van Golk?"

"Achille? Why should he kill Louis? *Mein Gott!* Achille had the most to lose by Louis dying. He cannot feed his fat face with Louis' cooking any more. No, *Inspektor.* There was only one man with the courage and imagination to have killed Louis. And that was Louis."

Detective Inspector Carmody rose from his chair. "I thank you for your help. We will be in touch as soon as there is something to report."

Hildegarde got up. "So I will never hear from you again?"

"I'm confident we'll be able to clear up this case."

"I'll send you a strudel when you do."

"Just one more question. When I called you this morning you said that *Gerechtigkeit* had been served."

"I loved my husband, Inspector. But what he did was wrong. He was wrong to make my Natasha a Greek tragedy. I told him that. But he wouldn't listen. Now he knows he was wrong. He has been punished."

"Indeed," he said softly. "And *justice* has been served."

"Precisely." Carmody hesitated for a moment, then opened the door for her.

"Mami!" Natasha rose from the bench in the corridor and ran to Hildegarde. The two women embraced, crying. They held tightly to one another. "Mami, Mami," Natasha repeated. Carmody stepped back from the doorway and stood listening as Natasha and Hildegarde sat on the bench.

"I didn't know what to do, Mami. I called you and Frau Muller told me you were here."

Hildegarde pulled back. "I did not want to see you."

"Mami, don't hate me. We only have each other now."

"We always had each other. Now we have nothing."

"I'll make it up to you, I swear I will."

"You owe me nothing."

"Mami, that first time, I made him do it. He was drunk."

"He told me. Please do not tell me again."

"You knew? You knew in Vienna?"

"*Tochter,* I knew before you knew. I could see it on your faces."

"Oh, God. How terrible it must have been for you."

"Yes. And now it will be terrible for you. I lost Louis a long time ago. You have just lost him, and I am sorry for you."

"I've always asked about you. Not from Louis, but from others. I've always known where you were." She smiled briefly. "I even knew about your fights with Miss Penreddy, and the time you sprained your arm, and when you flew to Paris to help Auguste start his restaurant. . . ."

"And I have watched you on the television, and I have read what you write in the magazines." There was a pause. The crying had stopped and they sat looking at one another, for a moment oblivious to where they were and why. "Do you remember, *Tochter,* how afraid you were that you would be ugly? Do you think back to those days at all?"

"Yes. I do. Mami, come with me."

"Where?"

"Everywhere! New York, San Francisco, Paris, Rome. I have a lot of money. We could open a restaurant together. Remember how we talked about it. How we tried to get Herr Schnederer to give us a lease on that place on the Opernplatz?"

Hildegarde moved away. "Please, don't do this to me. Do not be cruel. I have found peace all these years because I have had no dreams."

"But, Mami. This would be real. We could have our own place. The way we want it to be."

"*Tochter,* I am not unhappy with my life. And I do not think you are so unhappy with yours or else you would not be so successful. The champagne must not expect sympathy because it is not cognac. You have done well. Don't become bourgeois and punish yourself for it."

"Then come and live with me. Be part of my life."

"No," she said softly. "My own life is too important."

"Mami, let me help. I want . . ."

"Listen to me, I have tried to hate you, *mein Tochter.* For years I tried, because I thought I should. I thought it would be proper. But I loved you when you were a child because I wanted to love you. Even when you were sleeping with my husband, I loved you." She stood up. "It is enough. You must understand that I love you, but I do not wish to see you again."

"Mami, I am all alone."

"Then you must learn to like yourself." She looked at her watch. "I must go. I am late for the sauerbraten."

Natasha stood watching as Hildegarde walked away. Inspector Carmody came into the corridor and brought Natasha into his office. Without speaking he opened a file drawer, took out a bottle of brandy and a glass. He poured a drink for her. She drank it without ever meeting his eyes.

"Would you like another?" She nodded yes. He poured again.

"Thank you," she said, taking the glass from him. "I thought on my way back down here that I could make it all up to her somehow. Or that she would at least be angry enough with me to comfort my own guilt. But I just feel so empty now. I don't feel anything, Inspector." Natasha looked up and noticed the picture of the Queen on the wall. She started to laugh. "It's all so absurd."

"What is?"

"Last night I felt like Cinderella. Inspector, what do I do? About the funeral. How do I . . . ?"

. "Mr. van Golk has already made arrangements. The body . . . the remains were released an hour ago."

"Thank God. Is there anything else?"

"No. We have your statement from this morning."

Natasha got up from her chair. "Inspector, do you think he suffered very much?"

He turned away from her. "The report shows that his hands were found clutching the inside latch."

"Oh, my God. But how did . . ."

"We believe that he was knocked unconscious before being put into the oven. There was a fracture on the skull. But it would appear that the oven was not turned on until after the body was put into it."

"You mean he regained consciousness while the oven was heating?"

"It would have taken about ten minutes for the temperature to rise sufficiently to have seared his lungs. But we believe he died from suffocation because the flames took all oxygen out of the oven."

"Oh, my God. Oh, Louis." Natasha ran from the room. "I'm going to be sick."

NEW SCOTLAND YARD

Division of Homicide

Case Report No.   3287   Date 10 Sept
Reporting Officer   D. I. Carmody

Description of Unusual Event:
  At approx. 7:30 Mr. Frank Sacristedes (47, Caucasian, 8 Happenworth Square) discovered the body of Louis Wilhelm Kohner, 58, inside the bread baking oven of the Savoy Hotel. Sacristedes, an assistant to Kohner, was checking an incoming order in the pan-

try when he became aware of the smell of something burning. According to Sacristedes this was not unusual because rodents sometimes get trapped in an oven. Although it was Sacristedes' job to turn on the oven each morning preparatory to baking the luncheon breads, he noticed that the oven was already on when he arrived shortly after 7. Sacristedes assumed that Kohner had turned on the oven himself. Sacristedes opened the oven door and found the body. Sacristedes said he knew it was Kohner immediately because of the ring on his finger (a signet ring with a crossed knife and spoon given to members of Les Amis de Cuisine, a professional club for chefs). Sacristedes slammed the oven door and ran screaming through the hotel dining room until he was subdued by the security staff.

The investigating police officer turned off the oven. He opened the door and found Kohner's hands clenched as though still clutching the bolt on the inside of the door. Kohner's stomach had exploded from the pressure within the oven. His face was not immediately recognizable until it was cleaned of internal debris. The deceased was twisted as though he were pushing from the inside to open the door (an impossibility). Identification of the body was almost immediate in view of the deceased's jewelry, keys, and watch. The mouth of the deceased was open wide as though he had been screaming. Verification of dental records reconfirmed the identity of the victim.

Examination showed that a blow had been dealt to the back of the skull. The blow (search at the scene indicated possible use of a heavy pot or wooden rolling pin) did not kill the victim but presumably rendered him unconscious while the perpetrator pushed the body into the oven. Analysis shows that the body was pushed in head first as evidence of blood was found at the back of the oven. This would indicate that the victim regained consciousness, moved himself to face the door, and tried to release himself from the oven.

The oven temperature (approx. 450 degrees) would indicate that the oven had been turned on just shortly before 7, only five or ten minutes before Mr. Sacristedes arrived. The coroner reports that death would have occurred due to suffocation. If not, when the oven temperature reached 200 degrees the air would have seared the victim's lungs. It would appear that death took place at about 7:10, some twenty minutes before the body was found.

Appended are the statement by Sacristedes, report from the police officer, report from the coroner.

Personal Observations:

A worrisome case. There appears to be a singular lack of motive for killing the deceased. The appended statements, while still unverified in some instances, appear to be accurate. Or, at least, do not conflict with my personal observations below.

H. Kohner: The deceased's wife had known for some time that her stepdaughter was sleeping with her husband. Why would she suddenly decide to kill him? Wouldn't it be easier to have killed her stepdaughter? It is possible she incinerated her husband before seven,

and was back in Brighton for my
call at eight. However, she does
not drive and would have required
an accomplice to drive her back
since the train schedules would
not accommodate her needs.

N. O'Brien: The deceased's stepdaughter.
Could something have happened
during the night she spent with
him? Perhaps he sought to end
their affair. Could be anger. Her
own guilt? Would appear to be
prime suspect, although we have
no evidence on which to hold her.

F. Sacristedes: Assistant to the deceased. Has no
supporting alibi, appears rather
unstable, but medical report indi-
cates his shock genuine. No apparent motive.

M. Ogden: The deceased's ex-son-in-law.
Clear motive in view of recent divorce and his wife's resumption of
her affair with the deceased. But
has corroborating alibi from pros-
titute (known to this department)
with whom he spent the night.

A. van Golk: Publisher of LUCULLUS Magazine.
Well known to the Royal Family.
Wife related to the Foreign Secre-
tary. Known to all the above. Had

employed the deceased on numerous occasions. Can produce no witness but claims he was asleep in his flat. Appears the most stable of the lot. There seems to be absolutely nothing he could gain from the death of the deceased.

atasha lay on the couch in Achille's office. Max kneeled at her side as Achille and Miss Beauchamp stood by. "Nat. It's me, Millie." She stirred. "Get her some water."

"Perrier," Natasha corrected before opening her eyes. "Did I die?"

"You fainted," Max said.

"In the elevator," she recalled. Miss Beauchamp brought the Perrier. Natasha sat up and clutched the glass. "I pushed my hand against the latch and imagined Louis was trying to open the oven door."

Achille broke the silence. "Beauchamp, bring the poor thing some halvah." Natasha smiled. "It's nothing," he said briskly. "We have our own halvah tree."

Natasha put her hand on Max's arm. "Hi, handsome. Long time no see."

"Two hundred and eleven days," he said.

Miss Beauchamp brought a tray with three more glasses of Perrier. "Downstairs does not drink with Upstairs," Achille said to her. "Smash the glass when you're finished."

Natasha stood up. She walked past Achille and stared out the window. "I keep thinking of Louis." She held on to herself to control the trembling. "I keep hearing him scream for help inside that oven."

"Dearest kumquat, there is no point in dwelling upon what has happened. Let's simply remember that Louis' *Pigeonneaux* last night was his own best epitaph."

"Is that the sum total of a man's life?" Natasha asked, turning to face Achille. "A goddamn hors d'oeuvre? Is that what you thought of Louis?"

"Indeed not, puss. I thought of Louis as a thoroughly dislikable beast. It was to his culinary credit, and to my unfailing good taste, that I overcame my abhorrence of his rancid Prussian temperament and gave him a pot in which to *petits pois.*"

"You were his friend, Achille," she reminded him. "You always helped him."

"As I would have helped Hitler had he been able to poach a decent *quenelle.*"

"Thank God I won't be around to hear what you say about me when I die."

"Ah, but that is quite a different story," Achille said. "When you die, my darling, I will no doubt be shattered. Possibly I shall even cancel my dinner plans. In memoriam to you, I shall have a spun-sugar tooth, the size of the Arc de Triomphe, implanted next to the grave of Shakespeare."

"And when I die?" Max asked.

"I shall have you embalmed under contract to Fortes. You shall be scrubbed and dressed in a suit the color of foreskin. Then I will have you wrapped in see-through plastic, hermetically sealed, and dropped into the Thames as the largest used prophylactic in the world."

Miss Beauchamp began coughing. "And when you die," Achille continued, "I shall simply cable Rudolf Hess."

"If you don't mind," Miss Beauchamp said, "I must excuse myself."

"An appropriate, but impossible, goal," Achille shouted after her.

"I keep wondering," Natasha began, "what kind of person could have done such a thing."

"Someone with flair, I should think," Achille said. "Or at least someone who hated the Savoy. Talk about infamy, do you know they had to run across the street begging crumpets from the Strand Palace? It's a *scandale* in the great tradition. As I understand it, the Savoy must replace its most venerable oven, to say nothing of replacing its most venerable cook."

"Louis left the flat at about a quarter past six," Natasha said. "He was off to shop at Covent Garden, and then to the Savoy."

"Then, after the Royal Health Service recertifies the kitchen, then, *mon Dieu,* the Savoy must recertify its own reputation."

"He usually arrived at the Savoy by seven-thirty. But this morning—my God"—she stopped for a moment—"was it only this morning? For some reason he never got to the market."

"Ah," Achille said, smiling, "the custards of Carême are curdling today."

Max ignored him. "Then, the first thing we need to know is why Louis went directly to the Savoy."

"Alimentary my dear Ogden," Achille said. "He went directly to the Savoy because either he was unable to go to the market or he never intended going."

"Or, he was talked out of going," Max said.

"That would be like talking the pip from an avocado," Achille said.

"He's right," Natasha said to Max. "No one could have talked Louis out of going to the market."

"Then perhaps he was knocked out as he left the flat," Max said.

"And a little girl rolled him downhill to the Savoy?" Achille asked.

"They could have had a car," Natasha said.

"But why take him to the Savoy to kill him?" Max asked. "Maybe someone did knock him on the head as he left the flat. But if they just wanted to rob him or even kill him, they would have done it right then and there."

"You think someone intended to kill him that way . . . the way they did?" Natasha asked.

"May we adjourn this meeting of Cretins Against Crime?" Achille asked. "Surely all this did he, didn't he, could he, would he is becoming tiresome."

"Tiresome?" Natasha yelled. "Achille, someone murdered my father."

"Your stepfather," Max corrected.

"Your lover," Achille gloated.

"You bastard," Natasha said.

"I?" Achille asked. "I who have seen to every detail? Indeed, I who planned a most tasteful memorial service for what's-his-name? I who even arranged for burial at St. Timothy's, which is more difficult to get into than Claridge's? I am even preparing a commemorative volume of Louis' recipes to be published for all his friends."

"A very limited edition," Max said.

"Too true. Perhaps we should distribute them among the sobbing throngs at his funeral."

"That'll shoot five copies," Max said.

"What time is the service?" Natasha asked angrily.

"That is of no concern to you. You will not be here. I have you booked on a flight to Rome this evening. There is a suite reserved at the Grand. Nutti writes that the leftists have been agitating for a national shutdown of the pasta factories. I knew you would want to do a story for one of your dreary radical feminist rags. Moreover, I promised Nutti I would someday devote a feature to his superb lobster mousse. Stay in Rome until you're due back here for the demonstration at Harrods."

"Achille, are you crazy? What world are you in? I don't want to go to Rome. Don't you understand how I feel? It's three o'clock in the afternoon. Yesterday at this time I was skinning oranges at Buckingham Palace. I don't know any more who or what I am."

"But I know precisely who and what you are. And what is best for you. Besides, I've gone to a great deal of trouble to have the BBC cover the Harrods demonstration on Wednesday. All of Britain is agog to see the beautiful Natasha O'Brien and her *Bombe Richelieu* on the telly. Now, come give me a kiss and go bye-bye on the big silver bird."

"I hate to say it, Nat, but Achille is right. There's nothing you can do here. You need some perspective."

"Goddamn it, I don't need perspective. I need time to cry. Why don't you just tell me to go out, buy a new hat, and forget it all? Don't you realize what I've been through? I was with Louis this morning. Only hours ago. Then the police station. Then I saw Hildegarde. And then, for the grand finale, I faint in the goddamn elevator and wake up in the arms of the man I divorced."

"See," Max said, "every cloud does have a silver lining." He sat down next to her. "All crap aside, I know how you feel."

Natasha began shaking her head, the tears falling freely. "No. No, you don't. You don't know anything about how I feel. You don't know anything." She looked up at him, the tears streaming down her face. "I never loved Louis."

"Of course you didn't," Achille said. "How could you? He never loved you. Louis loved only his *Frau.* You both merely enacted, with consent of the law,

78

your mutual Oedipal fantasies. You were very fortunate indeed to have the forbidden dream of every young girl come true."

"Achille," she whispered.

"Yes, my love?"

"Stop reading those penny dreadfuls." Natasha blew her nose and then walked once around the room as Achille and Max watched her silently. "All these years I've dreaded the day I would meet Hildegarde. And I was right. If only she had let me . . ."

"Natasha, my darling," Achille said, "the Pharaoh did not make blintzes for Moses."

The telephone rang and Achille picked it up. "I told you no calls. Very well. Hello, darling doctor. And how is London's leading necrophiliac today? Are you trying to sell me tickets to the proctologists' ball? Well, then what? I have never been better. No, I haven't forgotten. Of course, I'm certain. As a matter of fact, I began my diet this very morning."

Natasha and Max left Achille's office. They stood on Curzon Street in the low orange of a setting sun.

"Let's at least have a cup of something," Max said. "For old times?" She nodded. They crossed over to Shepherd's Market and sat down at a table in front of a *trattoria.* Max ordered two espressos.

"How have you been?" she asked.

"You mean since dearth did us part? That's a heavy question."

"I mean, has it been very hard for you?"

"No." He smiled. "It's mainly been hard for *you.*"

"Millie!"

"Well, what the hell do you want me to tell you? You wake up one morning, look me in the eye while we're taking a shower, and tell me you want a divorce. I rub your back and ask you why. You rub my back and tell me you don't know why. We get dressed. We have coffee. You go to your office and I go to mine. I come home, the place is cleaned out, and you're gone."

"I only took what was mine."

"You didn't take *me.*"

"I took what was my property," she said.

"None of it was your property. It was ours. You can't divide *ours* into *yours* and *mine.* Ours is ours is ours."

"No. Things is things is things. That's all they were, Millie. Just things that have no meaning."

"No meaning?" he asked. "Do you know I cried over the silverware? That was *our* silverware in the drawer. And all of a sudden I had half a set. Service for six. We didn't *each* own six settings. We each owned *twelve* settings."

"Millie, we never owned each other."

"You did. You owned me, babe."

"Maybe that was the problem. But I don't own you any more."

"No, you liberated us both. You got what you wanted and I got corn flakes and bananas, Cokes, Yankee Doodles, frozen strawberries, powdered soups, canned peas, and whipped margarine."

"Millie, it's a real sickness with you."

"You know, in the six months since we stopped

rubbing each other's backs, I've tripled my use of plastic garbage bags."

"You've been eating those, too?"

"I think that was our problem. Insufficient garbage."

"We had plenty of garbage," she said defensively.

"We had terrible garbage. Anyone who looked through our garbage would have thought we were living in Warsaw. We never had really good American garbage, Nat. We never had cardboard boxes, or tin cans, or even little cartons from the Chinese retaurant. It's a good thing the CIA never looked through our garbage."

"Not that I haven't thoroughly enjoyed reminiscing with you about our garbage," she said, getting up, "but someone rather dear to me was murdered this morning and I'm fleeing the country, you see. I have a plane to catch."

"Why were you sleeping with Louis again?"

"I'm sorry, Millie. But now's not the time for that. I need a friend, not an ex-husband."

"I don't want to be an ex-husband."

She smiled and put her hand on his. "The only alternative is friend."

"All right, friend. But only because I feel sorry for you."

"Me, too."

"How can I help?" he asked.

"I don't know. I really wish you could."

"Let me take you to the airport."

"No."

"When will I see you again?"

"I don't know. Catch the show at Harrods next week."

"Nat, I'm really sorry."

"Darling, haven't you been reading your candy wrappers? Being in love means never having to say you're sorry. *Ciao*, Big M."

Fitipaldi, Montebianco e Toscapetti
Relazioni Pubbliche / Pubblicità / Pubblicitario

in Englich

Roma, 11 Sett

EGUAL PAY FOR EGUAL PASTA

Today came to Rome a new champion for egual
rights for women. Natasha O'Brien, the American
artist of food, flied in especially to meet with the
workers in the Maladente Macaroni Factory. She
was wore a tomato-coloured dress and bright zuc-

chini colour shoes. A woman of good beauty, she flied especially from London when she learned that the ziti division of MMF was getting a rise in pay but the all-women spaghetinni section got no rise.

Aldo Maladente spoke to reporters from his home near Verona. He told them it was all a lie.

Mss. O'Brien (who is not the daughter of the great Pat O'Brien) spoke to the women who marched outside the factory. "Basta il pasta" (Stop the macaroni), they called for over 18 hours. Joining in the marching, Mss. O'Brien said over international satellite televisione that she was "Goddamn mad" and that she sported the cause of the spaghetinni workers. "Why they should get less lire?" she asked. "It's as hard to make spaghetinni as it is to make the ziti."

Aldo Maladente spoke to reporters from his home near Verona. He told them ziti was harder.

Stella Fubini, leader of the striking spaghetinni workers, said that it was harder to make spaghetinni because it was more fragile than "the fat pig ziti." Fubini urged all Italian women to stop serving pasta for 49 hours (two days). She reminded all Italian women that in China they live without pasta and the Cultural Revolution was a successful because the workers fought against fascist regimes by eating only rice.

Mss. O'Brien told how pasta came from China in Marco Polo to Italy. Fubini told the crowd that ziti did not come from China but was a product of the fascists to see that men had more pay than the women. Everybody cheered. Fubini told that the flag of Italy red, white and green was red for tomatoes, white for garlic, and green for peppers. "We do not need pasta to be great," she said. "The people of Italy should unite under their peppers until the fascist rats give us the same pay they give the men for ziti."

Mss. O'Brien said she would come back again, and she said she would in person make a telephone call to the factory owner.

Aldo Maladente spoke to reporters from his home near Verona. He said "yankee go home."

atasha gazed across the Piazza Navona from her table at Tre Scalini. The waters from the Bernini fountains, and the cool breeze that insinuated its way through the streets from the Tiber, contributed to her sense of well-being. And isolation. London was the distant planet of Tuesday. She was on Thursday.

The tourists, like a swarm of maggots following a well-worn path, were nearly all gone. Rome again belonged to the Italians. And to the Germans, whose year-round presence constituted a peacetime occupation.

"Ouch!" Natasha turned from the fountains and

faced Nutti Fenegretti, whose grip on her hand had tightened.

"*Scusi, cara,*" he said, raising her hand to his lips. "But I cannot bear to share you, even with the great Bernini."

Natasha smiled. She looked across the table at Nutti and squeezed his hand as tightly as she could.

"*Più, più, più,*" he whispered, encouraging her.

She smiled again. It was impossible not to smile at Nutti. He was a small man, about five foot three, with a thick head of black curly hair, a thick black mustache, and the shadow of a very heavy beard over his dark skin. Although in his fifties, Nutti was lean and muscular. He wore a tight-fitting tan suit, and the collar of his open dark-green shirt lay flat over the lapels of his jacket. A mass of dark curly hair pushed out from the neck of his shirt. The thing that made Nutti comical was that he had no eyebrows. He had lost them years ago in a pizza oven in Ferrara.

For over an hour they discussed Louis. Nutti cried openly, recounting how he first met Louis in Vienna, how Louis got him a job at the Rot Schinken. Nutti lived in Vienna for six months, staying with Louis and Hildegarde as often as he was thrown out of his rooming house for not paying his rent. He would spend all his money on custom-made clothes. Natasha remembered Hildegarde's shock, when doing his laundry, to find that his underwear was hand-made.

By the time Louis left Vienna, Nutti was already in Paris and helped Louis find work there, then in Brussels, and, eventually, in Brighton. Nutti had always been Her Uncle, someone who periodically turned up drunk, or else sent an extravagant gift whenever he felt like declaring a holiday. Natasha had seen him often through the years, each time growing more uneasy that Nutti would someday verbalize the thoughts she could read in his eyes.

"Come with me now," he said, looking at his watch. "I shall make you forget everything."

Natasha looked down at his plate. The scaloppine was untouched. "You haven't eaten a thing," she said. "And I've been gorging myself."

"You think I would eat here?" he asked. "Nutti eats only what Nutti cooks. I do not eat from Giuseppe's kitchen."

"Then why did you order?"

"If I did not order he would think I was not hungry. Now he will know." Nutti looked at her and smiled. He waved his hand across the untouched cannelloni, scaloppine, peppers, and the mushroom salad. "His especialties."

Natasha laughed. "You're crazy."

"I am only crazy for you." He looked at his watch. "Come with me, Natasha. I will make glorious love to you."

"More Pellegrino, please," she said, raising her glass. He looked at her as he began pouring.

"Our bodies were meant to be together. I am *fantastico* in bed. You will love touching me. Those slender hands of yours . . ." He took her hand and began kissing her fingers. "I long to have them moving down my stomach."

"Nutti," she began.

"I will kiss your nipples as the sun kisses the ripening *pomodoro*."

"I want dessert."

"You do not need dessert. Your dessert shall be the moment of ecstasy when I am between your silken thighs and I enter your body."

"That wasn't what I had in mind. I want a *Tartuffo*."

"I am better than *Tartuffo*," he said, slamming his hand on the table. "You talk of *gelati* when I offer you magic." He looked at his watch. "I am starving. Come with me. And then, after I have been deep, deep inside you and your hands are weak from clutching at my back, begging me to stop, then, I will feed you spumoni from my fingers."

She put her hand under the table and rested it on his knee. "*Domani*, Nutti," she said. "After you have eaten, and when I am hungry."

"But tomorrow I am not working."

"Then we'll have the whole day."

He looked at her and shrugged his shoulders. "You are giving up the chance of our lifetimes," he said, glancing at his watch again.

"*Domani*, Nutti," she said. *"Per piacere."*

"Then tomorrow you shall eat nothing. I will make love to you six times. *Antipasto, zuppa, pasta, pesce, carne,* and *il dolce.* It will be the most glorious experience of your life. And then, afterward, I shall cook my *Aragosta* for you. You will take notes for Achille."

"On which dish?"

"On which you like the most," he said, smiling as he got up. *"Domani, il miracolo."* He kissed her hand. "I must go to my mistress, *la cucina.* Otherwise half of Dusseldorf will go hungry. We shall begin at noon tomorrow. Before lunch."

Natasha smiled. "Your place or mine?"

"Mine, of course. The cook does not fry eggs in the hen house." He snapped his fingers and the waiter brought him the check. Nutti signed it, waved his arm across the uneaten food, smiled, and said, *"I miei complimenti al Maestro."* He bent down to kiss Natasha, slipped his hand quickly from one breast to the other, shouted *"Ciao,"* and left.

The waiter came over to clear the table. *"Dolci? Frutta?"* he asked.

"Grazie, no. Niente." Then, feeling very much alone, *"Sì, piacere, cappuccino."* She looked again at the fountains and imagined strollers in Renaissance costumes. Then she pictured World War II GI's. Perhaps her own father. Had he once stared at the same fountains? Could he have imagined that someday his own child would be staring into them looking for his reflection?

Natasha had no place to go. She lingered in the Piazza Navona until she began getting second nods from the same men, and then she walked along the Corso Vittorio Emanuele in the direction of the Forum. In her mind she saw all the blank boxes on her month-at-a-glance calendar. She had worked so hard to keep those boxes clear, imagining how they would be filled with notations about dinners with Louis, kitchens they had discovered, places they wanted to go. She could not put her *domani* with Nutti on that same page.

It was still lunchtime and the streets were quiet except for the noise from the *ristoranti* and *trattorie* that bulged with loud conversation and the clang of silverware. Of all the cities in Europe, she liked

Rome the best for walking. There were hills and steps and piazzas and alleys. The city was like a grand buffet after the first go-round. Some of the good stuff still remained for those who knew what the good stuff was.

As she approached the Via dei Fori Imperiali, she woke a sleeping old man to buy a cup of chocolate ice. Then she walked up the steps to the Campidoglio and looked down on the Forum, trying to fit her life into the historical perspective spread before her. She leaned on the balustrade, sipped at her ice, and began to cry.

Who were the tears for, she wondered. For Papa Louis? For her lover? For Natasha O'Brien perhaps. Perhaps. She stared at the graveyard of ancient Rome as though she were looking into her own future. Someday her child might stand in that spot wondering if Natasha had ever been there. Clearly not an original thought for Natasha's child. Clearly not an original grief for Natasha. Originality belonged to the Bernini fountains, because they were permanent, uninvolved with the weeping and wondering of children. Oh, Louis. She crushed the empty paper cup in her hands and threw it at a broken column. How elitist, she thought, to vent her anger by littering in the Forum.

It was after five when she returned to the Grand, now determined to fill in the blank spaces in her calendar. She asked the desk clerk for her key.

"Giorno," he muttered, stepping back. Two policemen appeared beside her. She felt their hands grip her arms.

"What is this?" she asked them. "Let go of me." Their hands tightened as she tried to free herself.

"I am sorry, *signorina*," the desk clerk whispered. *"Polizia."*

"You're hurting me," she said, trying to free herself from them. There was suddenly a crowd around her.

"They wish you to go with them," the clerk said.

"I don't wish to go," she shouted.

"Please, *signorina*," he said as the police began pushing her through the lobby.

"Call the American Embassy," she called to the clerk. "Stop it, what are you doing?" she screamed at the police.

"Per piacere," one of them said as they forced her through the door and over to a police car. A third officer got out of the car, opened the door, and Natasha was pushed into the back seat between the two men who had taken her from the lobby. They slammed the doors and the driver started the car. He turned on the siren and they began racing through the streets.

"Where are you taking me?" she asked. *"Dove? Dove? Dove?"* she repeated. The car raced through the streets, at times seemingly ahead of its own bleating siren. She looked through the windows and saw faces turning to look at her. They drove into the Piazza Barberini, and onto the Via del Corso. "I am an American citizen," she yelled. "You have the wrong person. I haven't done anything. Where are you taking me?" She was breathing heavily, inhaling the underarm odors of her captors. "Where the fuck are you taking me?" she screamed.

"Per piacere," the one on her right said.

There was no point in struggling; they were stronger. And there was no point in yelling; they couldn't understand her. She sat between them thinking it didn't matter where they were taking her; they would crash before arriving anywhere. The driver never slowed down, always making the motorists and pedestrians swerve, slam their brakes, run, and shout. They must be taking her to the police station, she thought. But where? And why?

She thought she recognized the section they were in, somewhere near the Piazza del Popolo. Somewhere near Nutti's restaurant. The car came to a screeching halt in a very narrow street. The siren finally stopped. The worst was over, she thought. The police helped her out of the car, still holding her arms as they led her into what appeared to be the back door of a restaurant. It was Nutti's restaurant. They pushed her past the cans of garbage and into the kitchen. They kept pushing her until she stepped on something. A fish. She looked at the floor and saw dead fish scattered about. Then out of the corner of her eye she saw something. Pink. Red. She looked again. The fish tank.

The water in the fish tank was red. Something hung over the side. An arm. A lobster was crawling on the arm. The rest of the body was submerged. Nutti's once comical face was pressed against the glass. His mouth and eyes were open as though calling for help.

Natasha relaxed into the grip the police had on her arm. They led her through the service area, and into the restaurant. The room was lit for cleaning; it would never have been that bright during service hours. Tables were piled high with chairs. The police led Natasha to a table, took the chairs off, and she sat down. Her eyes focused on the table next to her. It was fully set with tablecloth, flowers, dishes, silverware, and crystal. Amid the sea of chair legs that surrounded him, a man sat eating. He nodded his head, rose for a moment, and then sat again.

"I hope you do not mind that I am eating," he said with an Italian accent. "But I am enjoying my meal very much. It is not very often that I eat in such places. The *tortellini* is superb. Tell me," he said, looking directly at her for the first time, "where have you been, Miss O'Brien?"

His eyes were ice blue. His face was smooth, olivey, and he looked as though he had no beard. He appeared to be in his late thirties. A very handsome man. He wore a dark-blue double-breasted suit, a light-blue shirt, and an orange tie with a very large knot.

"Who are you?" she asked softly.

"I am Capitano Gilli. I am of the police. I wish to know where you have been."

"Who did it?"

"I did not," he replied as he ate.

"You think I did?"

"Where have you been, Miss O'Brien?"

"Walking."

"You were with someone?"

"I was alone."

"Perhaps someone saw you. You stopped in a shop?"

"No."

"Perhaps you asked for directions?"

"You think I did it?"

"I am asking where you have been." He put down his fork and pushed his plate away. "Would you like some wine?" he asked as he refilled his glass.

She looked at him for a moment. Then she looked at the empty room, at the door to the kitchen through which she had just come.

"Why did you have me brought through there?"

"Tell me where you have been."

"None of your business." She stood up. "I want to go."

"Sit down, Miss O'Brien."

"I want to go. I want to get out of here."

"Sit down," he shouted. "You are being questioned by the police in the murder of Nutti Fenegretti. You are suspected of knocking him unconscious on the back of the head, of pushing him into the water and drowning him. You are suspected of taking a large knife, smashing his head open, and then splitting him down the back the way one does a lobster."

Natasha sat down.

"Cameriere!" he shouted. The waiter ran into the room and cleared the table. *"Due caffè, per piacere."* The waiter left quickly. Natasha sat immobile, staring into space. She thought of looking down at the Forum, of having found some perspective.

The waiter brought two cups of coffee and put one

on each table. Natasha looked at Gilli. "Thank you," she said.

"*Prego.*" There was a pause, and then he began, "You understand I must ask you questions?"

"Yes."

"*Bene.* Then, may I begin?"

Natasha looked at him. "Who found the body?"

"Palmestri, the waiter . . ." He stopped, realizing he was answering her questions.

"They don't open until seven," she said. "What was he doing here?"

"He says that he is innocent. That he came early only to steal some fish for his family. Miss O'Brien, *I* am supposed to be asking the questions."

"Who else was in the restaurant?"

"The baker came at four o'clock to make the pasta in his kitchen," he said, getting angrier with each word. "Fenegretti was in the other kitchen. The baker and Fenegretti have not spoken to each other in years. They hated one another. The waiters do not come until six o'clock. The assistant cooks do not come until five o'clock. Fenegretti comes promptly at half past two."

"Well, what about the baker?"

"It is my opinion that the baker hated Fenegretti too much to kill him."

"*Hated* him too much to kill him?"

"Exactly. You do not understand Italians. Finding someone you can really hate is as important as finding someone you really love. You must have them both in your life. You do not suddenly kill someone you have spent years hating. You have an investment in that person. You kill someone for a reason, or for no reason. You do not kill because of hate."

"Then who did it?"

Gilli looked at Natasha. "Where have you been, Miss O'Brien?"

"I had lunch with Nutti. He left at around two-thirty. I walked twice around the Piazza Navona. I walked to the Forum. I stopped for some ice. I went to the Campidoglio. I ate my ice. I looked at the Forum. I left the Campidoglio. I took a taxi and went back to the Grand."

"Mille grazie," he said. "Then you are innocent."

"Clearly."

"Then I shall call Inspector Carmody and . . ."

"Carmody?"

"Yes. You remember Inspector Carmody?"

"How do you know him?"

"I have never had the pleasure of meeting him. But we are colleagues. I received from him a call. He told me about the incident in London, and that you were coming to Rome."

"To warn you in case anyone was murdered in Rome? Or in case any banks were held up?"

"No. To ask me to have your activities . . ."—he stumbled for the gentlest word—"observed."

"Observed? Then he suspects me of killing Louis?"

"It is his job."

"To suspect me of killing Louis? That stupid bastard. That pasty-faced weasel called to warn you that I was coming to Rome? To follow me?"

"And then someone kills Fenegretti. An unfortunate coincidence."

"That's quite an epitaph." She looked at Gilli. How could someone that handsome think she was a criminal? "I would like something to drink."

"Cinzano, Sambucca, whiskey, Fiuggi?"

"Pellegrino. I never drink Fiuggi," she said. "It has no bubbles."

"I do not like bubbles."

She said without smiling, "I know. They tickle your nose."

He shrugged his shoulders, and called to the waiter for one Pellegrino and one Fiuggi. Natasha sat back. "I can't go through it all again. I really don't think I can."

The waiter brought the two bottles of mineral water. He put the Pellegrino in front of Gilli, and the Fiuggi in front of Natasha. Gilli smiled. He watched as Natasha put the glass to her lips. She winced, and looked down at the bottle.

"Police brutality," he said softly, exchanging the glasses.

"Why don't you take him out of there?" she asked, pointing to the kitchen. She raised her head as she felt the tears stream down her cheek.

"I was only waiting for you."

"For me?"

"For your reaction. My business is one of interpreting reactions."

"Well then, how do you interpret this?" She threw her drink in his face.

He stood up, laughing, and took a napkin to dry himself. "I think that is a good sign."

"Don't laugh," she said angrily. "Don't you laugh. Your business is not to take advantage of me. How dare you. How dare you have me dragged out of my hotel? How dare you make me walk through that kitchen? You goddamn bastard, who the hell do you think you are? Do you know who I am? How dare you accuse me of killing Nutti? Nutti was . . ." She stopped for a moment. "He was . . . was, was, was. Why is everyone in my life becoming a was?"

"He was a friend?" Gilli asked as he sat down at her table.

"More," she replied quietly.

"You were lovers?"

"Almost." She smiled. "He was to make love to me six times tomorrow."

"Six times?"

"Antipasto, zuppa, pasta, pesce, carne, dolce."

"While you eat he was to make love to you?"

"No. It was just a game. A silly game."

"But I must tell you," he said excitedly, "that is my diet. Each time I make love I think of *cannelloni, lasagna, fettucini, manicotti.* And I do not eat those things any more. I have lost twenty kilos while I make love. My stomach is now flat," he said, patting his stomach. "I have thought it should be a book."

"You should call it *Just Another Fucking Diet.*"

He began to laugh. "I am sorry. I have never heard an American lady use that word."

"What word? Fuck?"

"Yes," he said. "Fuck."

She looked at him for a moment. "Fuck," she said simply. Then, slowly, and without emotion, "Fuck. Fuck. Fuck. Fuck."

"You are right," he said. "It is not so funny."

They sat quietly for a moment.

"What will you do now?" she asked.

"I will take you back to your hotel."

"Am I under arrest?"

"For what?"

"It's very clear. I flew from New York to London to kill Louis on Tuesday. Then I flew from London to Rome to kill Nutti on Thursday. I am the only person who has been in both places."

"Then I shall have to watch you very closely."

"Can you take me out of here?"

"Where do you wish to go?"

"The hotel."

"Of course. You wish to be alone."

"No," she said. "I do not wish to be alone."

"You are emotionally upset."

"Yes."

"You are grieving."

"Yes."

"You are frightened."

"Yes."

"Bellissima," he whispered.

The telephone rang. Natasha awoke and raised her head from the pillow. She leaned across Gilli's chest and reached for the receiver on the night table.

"Hello?"

"Miss Natasha O'Brien, please. Paris is calling."

Gilli stirred. "For me?" he asked sleepily.

"No," she said. "Yes, operator, I am Natasha O'Brien."

Gilli moved his hand under the sheet and began to caress her breast.

"Nat? Nat? It's me, Millie."

"Millie? Did you hear?" she asked.

Gilli began to pinch her nipples. She traced the outline of his lips with her finger.

"The chef at the American Embassy called me. I couldn't believe it. Are you all right?"

Gilli put his mouth to her nipples and rubbed them with his tongue. Natasha breathed in sharply.

"Yes. I think so."

"You sound terrible, Nat." Gilli's hands were moving across her body. "You must be going through hell," Max said.

Natasha began to pinch Gilli's nipples. "You wouldn't believe what I'm going through now," she said. Gilli's hand pushed her legs apart. "It's incredible."

"Listen, Nat, you've got to get out of there. How much can you take?"

Natasha held Gilli's penis in her hand. "I don't know. Not too much more."

"Then for Chrissake get on the next plane, and meet me in Paris."

Gilli was on top of her, entering with force. "Oh," she said.

"I know," Max replied. "It must be more than you can bear."

"Oh, my God, yes. Yes."

"Nat, it's breaking my heart to hear you this way." Gilli was rocking rapidly. Natasha put her arm around his neck and held tightly to him. "Nat, when can you get here?"

"I'll come as fast as I can," she said, rocking with Gilli.

"Is that a promise?" Max asked. "I want to be with you, Nat. I know how alone you must be. It must be so hard for you."

"Yes," she breathed into the receiver.

"Nat, you sound really bad. How soon can you come?"

"I'm coming," she whispered.

"When?" Max asked.

"Now, now, right now, as I'm talking to you. Oh, Millie, it's unbelievable."

"Nat, don't let yourself go like that. Please. Pull yourself together. Please. It'll be all right. I promise you."

Gilli withdrew but remained on top of her.

"Where are you?" she asked.

"The Plaza. How soon can you leave?"

Natasha looked at Gilli. "How soon can I leave?" she repeated. He shrugged his shoulders as he put his arms around her. "I don't know," she said. "I'm being held by the police." Gilli smiled.

"Why? They can't hold you. You can leave anytime. Call the Consulate."

"I can leave anytime?" she repeated, looking at Gilli. He nodded yes. "I thought perhaps I should stay awhile," she said to Max. Gilli nodded his head no, and lay back at her side. "But, you're right, there's no reason to stay. I'll leave tonight."

"I'll meet you. What plane?"

"I don't know. Don't meet me. I'll come to the Plaza."

"I'll wait for you. And Nat?"

"Yes?" she asked.

"I love you," Max said.

Natasha handed the phone to Gilli. He put the receiver to his mouth, and kissed it loudly. Then he hung up.

Dipartimento di Giustizia
Divisione di Roma
Ufficio di Omicidio

12 Settembre

TO: Detective Inspector Carmody
FROM: Capitano L. Gilli
RE: Nutti Fenegretti

As per your telephone request I enclose for you copies of reports concerning the death of Sr. Fenegretti, including the statement of Miss Natasha O'Brien.

After a personal in-depth examination of Miss O'Brien, I cannot agree with your suspicions concerning her being a possible murder suspect. I do not believe this lady capable of murder. Besides, I have rarely found female killers to be as clever as Miss O'Brien. It is my experience that women who kill do so in a moment of passion. Your suspicion that the same person who killed L. Kohner also killed Sr. Fenegretti cannot be substantiated. I personally believe that Miss O'Brien was by coincidence in both cities at the times of the murders.

Even as we did not have the airtight alibi of Abruzzio Cenelli (the man who sold Miss O'Brien in the ice), I could not uncover, in my investigation of Miss O'Brien, any possible motive for her to murder Sr. Fenegretti.

Since we cannot presume that the death of Sr. Fenegretti had obvious benefits for any radical political groups or for any criminal organizations, and since the method of his death does not fit the patterns of any known or suspected criminals, we have decided not to assign personnel to this case.

The official opinion then, at this time, is that somebody crazy came into the restaurant and killed him.

he black Phantom stopped. Rudolph got out and walked briskly around the front of the car as he checked his watch. He opened the back door with one hand and thrust the other inside to help Achille.

"Right on time for your flight, sir," Rudolph said, pulling him to a standing position.

"My case."

Rudolph reached to the back seat and took the thin black briefcase with AVG engraved in gold above the latch. "Have a pleasant day, sir. I hope Mrs. van Golk is feeling better."

Achille nodded and entered the terminal building. He walked directly to the Swissair counter.

"Good morning, Mr. van Golk," the clerk said. "Must be Thursday."

"Good morning." He handed her his ticket and passport. She picked up the telephone.

"Mr. van Golk is here. Will you have the courtesy car at Gate 11, please? Thank you." She hung up the receiver and gave him back his passport and ticket with a boarding pass. "Seats 1A and 1B as usual." She smiled. "Have a pleasant trip."

"Good day," he said without smiling. He turned and walked past the newsstands, the gift shops, and the clusters of tourists. As he approached the line at passport control, he was motioned ahead by one of the inspectors. It was at best a superfluous gesture, since Achille always walked to the head of any line.

"Good morning, Mr. van Golk," the inspector said. "Is it Thursday already? A nice sunny morning it is."

Achille handed him his British passport. "Good morning."

"You'll be soon needing another one of these. Have a good day." He stamped the passport and handed it back.

"Thank you. Good day." Achille walked in a straight line through the international lounge, past the duty-free shops and down the corridor to Gate 11, where he was greeted by yet another smiling face.

"Good morning, Mr. van Golk," the young girl said as she took his boarding pass. "A lovely morning, isn't it?"

He walked slowly down the steps to where a car was waiting.

"Good morning, Mr. van Golk. Lovely morning, isn't it?" the driver said without turning around.

"Good morning." They drove slowly across the field, passing buses stuffed with executives carrying bottles of Scotch, and merry widows clutching make-up cases and fur coats. The car stopped directly in front of the ramp leading into the first-class cabin. Achille got out, and with great care walked slowly up the steps. He could feel the metal stairs moving from side to side and by the time he reached the top he was nearly out of breath. Miss Schnee held out her hand.

"If you tell me it's a lovely morning," he said to her, "I shall report you for exposing your genitalia over Luxembourg."

"I am so glad to see you." She took his arm and led him into the cabin. And then, in a pouting little-girl voice, "I was beginning to worry about you. It just wouldn't be Thursday without you."

The center armrest between seats 1A and 1B had already been removed. Miss Schnee held Achille's briefcase as he lowered himself into one and a half seats. She leaned across Achille to fasten the window half of 1A's seat belt to the aisle half of 1B's seat belt. "There, I bet we're nice and comfy now," she said, careful to press her breasts against his arm. "You naughty boy," she whispered.

"Would you be kind enough to bring me my Perrier?"

"Oh, Perrier, Perrier. I tasted that Perrier. It's nothing. Why don't you let yourself go and have a Coke? C'mon."

"Had I been on the *Lusitania*, and all the lifeboats were filled and gone, and were I standing on the deck as the ship was sinking and the captain told me that if I drank but one Coca-Cola, not only would the ship right itself and stay afloat, but also the drowned would be resurrected, I would pretend not to have heard him."

"Perrier?"

"Thank you." Achille looked at his watch. Ten minutes to ten. They were due to leave at ten and arrive in Geneva by eleven-fifteen.

"Fasten your seat belts, please. We are about to land at Cointrin Airport, Geneva. Please observe the no smoking sign. . . ."

"I didn't have the heart to wake you," Miss Schnee said as she tightened the knot on his tie. "I adore your tie. Polka dots are my very favorite. They're so masculine."

"Take this before we crash," he said, pointing to the half-empty bottle of Perrier. "I don't want to get my suit wet."

"You see? You do need someone to take care of you. Oh, I hope your wife is feeling better and can leave that nasty clinic. It's such a waste for a man like you to be all alone." He checked his watch. Ten past eleven. "Will I see you tonight on the return?" she asked.

"Unless you're grounded for vaginal odor, I would presume so."

"You. Really!" She pinched his arm and walked to the back of the cabin.

Achille was the first to descend the ramp and enter the terminal. He walked as rapidly as he could, but his leg hurt and he winced with each step. As he approached Swiss immigration, he was greeted with a smile.

"Good morning, Mr. van Golk," the officer said, taking his passport. "How are you today?"

"I am very well," he said. The passport was stamped and handed back to him.

"Have a good day."

"Thank you." Achille put the passport into his pocket as he continued walking past the crowds at the baggage carrousels, and over to the customs officer.

"Good day, Mr. van Golk," the customs man said.

"Good day." Achille raised his briefcase to signify he had nothing to declare. He walked through the impatient crowd of people waiting for familiar faces. He looked back once over his shoulder. Instead of leaving the terminal, he turned and walked to the baggage lockers in the departure lounge. He placed his briefcase in a locker, closed the door, and put the key in his vest pocket. He walked to the Alitalia ticket counter.

"I have a reservation on Flight 433 to Rome."

"Yes, sir. I'll check that for you. They're almost ready to board. May I have your passport, please?" the young man asked.

"Yes." Achille reached into his breast pocket and took out a Swiss passport. He handed it to the clerk, who was already dialing the phone.

"Was that economy or first class?"

"Economy," Achille answered, lowering his eyes.

"Did you wish a return . . . excuse me," and then into the phone, "Confirming a single in economy on four three three, the name is Victor, v-i-c-t-o-r, first name Hugo." While he was waiting for a reply, he again asked Achille if he wished a round-trip ticket.

"No. One way."

"Thank you," he said into the receiver and then put down the phone. He reached under the counter for a ticket as he looked at the clock above him. "Any luggage?" he asked.

"No."

"Good. How will you be paying, Mr. Victor? Card or cash?"

"Cash." Achille reached into his pocket and paid in Swiss francs.

"That will be Gate 32B. They'll be boarding in about five minutes."

"Thank you," Achille said. He took back his Swiss passport and ticket.

"Have a good flight, Mr. Victor."

Achille went to a telephone booth and stepped inside. He dialed the clinic.

"Dr. Enstein, please," he said to the receptionist.

"Dr. Enstein's office," another voice said.

"Dr. Enstein, please," he said.

"Who is calling, please?"

"Hugo Victor."

"Just one moment, please."

"Hello. Enstein here."

"This is Hugo Victor."

"I understand. May I call you back?"

"I told you I would never call unless I was actually here," Achille said sharply.

"I know, but may I have your number, please?"

"54-44-76." Achille hung up and waited. The phone rang.

"Please don't be offended," Dr. Enstein said. "I wanted to use my private line."

"How is she?"

"She expects you."

"Of course. And your staff expects to see me as well. That's why you must take her out of the clinic for the afternoon as though you were meeting me."

"I understand."

"I am wearing a dark-blue suit and a blue polka-dot tie. You met me with your car. The three of us had lunch together. Probably in that dreadful café she likes on the lakefront. We had an overdone trout with a rather remarkable Piesporter. Then we went for a drive in the country."

"I understand."

"How is your research coming?"

"It will take more money."

"I told you that would be no problem."

"The results are quite encouraging. Except . . . except I find this deception very disturbing."

"Doctor, my wife has been in your care for over a decade. It is more than thirteen years since I have shared my bed with her. Surely you would not deny me a few stolen hours of anonymous sexual pleasure in a country where I am not known. Especially when I am willing to pay so generously for it."

"Oh, you've been most generous. It's just the secrecy and intrigue that bothers me."

"Having grown up in a neutral country, I would have presumed secrecy and intrigue to be second nature."

"Please do not be facetious."

"Doctor. I have explained to you that if my wife's family were aware of my dalliances they would take action to prevent my drawing upon her inheritance. And then, Doctor, what could you draw upon for your research?"

"Your point is clear. You may rest assured I will take care of everything."

"I am confident you will, Doctor."

"Thank you."

"Good-bye." Achille hung up the receiver. He continued through the departure lounge to passport control, where he assured himself that no one from the later shift was on duty. He handed the Swiss passport to an inspector who stamped it and did not say hello.

"Merci," Achille said and then proceeded to Gate 32B, where he handed his ticket and passport to the clerk. He was given an economy boarding pass and was told to select his own seat once aboard. He walked under the metal detector, onto the boarding sleeve, and then into the plane. He squeezed himself into a right aisle seat so that he could extend his left leg into the aisle. A middle-aged German couple on their first trip to Rome sat next to him. They had spread between them a large map and were marking the routes they would walk, and planning how much time to spend. Why twenty minutes at the Spanish steps? Ten minutes at Trevi? Surely not more than half an hour for the Forum.

His presence was acknowledged only when he refused the cold meats and cheese served for lunch. By the time the plane began its descent to Fiumicino Airport, the German couple had decided two days was too long to be in Rome.

Achille got off the plane and made his way into the bus that waited on the airfield. He looked at his watch. It was one-fifteen. The timing was perfect. The bus threaded its way across the field to the international arrivals building.

He walked briskly to the head of the line at passport control. *"Permesso! Ufficiale,"* he whispered to the man at the front and, without waiting for a reply, stepped ahead of him and handed the inspector his Swiss passport.

Upon leaving the terminal, Achille hailed a taxi. "Piazza del Popolo," he said, handing the driver 40,000 lire. *"Presto, presto, presto."* The driver nodded, half saluted him in the rearview mirror, and started with such force that Achille was thrown back against the rear of the seat. They made the forty-five-minute drive into Rome in about thirty-five minutes. As soon as they came to the Piazza, Achille called, *"Qui, qui. Bene."* He waited until he was certain the driver was out of sight and then hailed another taxi. He gave an address only a short distance away. When they arrived, Achille paid the fare, careful not to overtip. He looked at his watch as he walked around the block. It was two-thirty. He stepped into a doorway and waited. After a few minutes he saw Nutti turn the corner, look at his watch, walk to the back door of the restaurant, unlock it, and step inside.

Achille crossed the street, turning his head to see whether anyone was watching him. He opened the door. Nutti stood a few feet away facing him.

"Non mi piace questo," Nutti said angrily. "I do not like this, my friend. Come in. What is the mystery?"

"Is anyone here?" Achille asked.

"No. What is this about? I have just left Natasha. I feel very unhappy to lie to her."

"You didn't lie," Achille said, looking around at the kitchen. "You just didn't tell her you were meeting me."

"But why? You make me very sad. I want to see my old friend, but I do not know why I must meet you this way."

"Nutti, you are a fine fellow," he said, looking at the fish tank. "And I have so few friends I can trust."

"You know you can trust me, Achille."

"I know. You are certain you told no one about my calling you?"

"My friend, you say to me on the telephone that if I tell anyone it will mean the end of you. And then you say it will mean the end of *me*. So tell me, Achille, did I tell anyone?"

"Good."

"But what is it? You are in some kind of trouble?"

"The worst kind."

"Dio," he whispered, putting his hand to his lips. *"Non è possibile."*

"Yes. It is true. I am dying."

"No."

"Yes."

"My God." Nutti began to cry. "First Louis and now you. And you came to tell me. You came to tell me yourself. I am very honored, Achille." He started to put his arms around Achille, but was pushed away.

"Please don't do that."

"I am sorry, Achille," Nutti said, drawing back quickly. "It hurts you? You are in pain? Did I hurt you? I did not mean to!"

"No, there is no pain."

"No pain? You are dying and there is no pain? How wonderful," he cried out, tears coming to his eyes. "But what is it, Achille? What is wrong with you?"

"I am too fat," Achille said slowly.

"Che cosa?"

"I am too fat."

Nutti sat down at the table. "You are dying of fatness?" he asked.

"Yes."

Nutti raised his hands in the air. He shrugged his shoulders in exasperation and turned away from Achille. "Then stop eating," he said.

Achille picked up a large frying pan and, holding it in both hands, swung it at the back of Nutti's head. Nutti slumped forward onto the table. Achille took a towel and wiped his fingerprints from the pan. He removed his jacket and took an ankle-length apron from a pile of fresh linen.

Achille grabbed Nutti under the arms and dragged him to the fish tank. He pushed Nutti's head down into the water. Nutti suddenly regained consciousness and desperately tried to raise his head, but Achille had both hands on his neck and was leaning hard on top of him. Nutti flailed his arms, choking and belching large bubbles of air. He knocked some fish onto the floor and then died.

Achille left him half hanging outside the tank and picked up a cleaver. With both hands he brought the cleaver down to split open the back of Nutti's head. Blood splattered onto his apron. He raised the cleaver again and split open the back of Nutti's neck.

As though it were food coloring, Nutti's blood ran into the fish tank and marbled the clear water. Achille brought the cleaver down again and again until he had finally split Nutti all the way down his back. He lifted the body and it slipped easily into the tank.

Achille went to the sink, washed the cleaver, and rubbed off his fingerprints. Carefully, he took off the long white apron and dropped it into the tank. He washed his hands, put on his jacket, and used his handkerchief to turn the knob on the outside door.

Achille strolled casually for a few blocks, trying not to limp despite the pain in his leg. He hailed a taxi and returned to the airport.

"Is that one way to Geneva, Mr. Victor?"

"Yes."

"Will that be charge or cash?"

"Cash," Achille said, paying in lire.

"Your flight will be loading at about ten to four, Gate 11."

"Thank you," Achille said, taking the ticket.

"Have a pleasant flight, Mr. Victor."

Upon landing in Geneva, Hugo Victor was processed through the arrivals-area second shift of immigration and customs inspectors before stepping outside the terminal into the cool air. A delightful climate. Achille van Golk re-entered the building and took his briefcase from the locker in the departure lounge. It was five-thirty. He walked quickly to the Swissair counter. The familiar evening shift was on duty. Achille nodded his head and smiled.

"Good evening, Mr. van Golk," the clerk said. Achille handed him his British passport and the return portion of his London-Geneva round-trip ticket. "How was your wife today?"

"About the same, thank you."

"Have a pleasant flight," he said, giving him a boarding pass. "See you next Thursday."

"Of course." Achille smiled and nodded his way through passport control. In the departure lounge he paused to look at the display of Swiss chocolates and then turned sharply toward Gate 21.

"Good evening, Mr. van Golk." The clerk behind the desk smiled and took his boarding pass. Achille walked through the jetway to the plane and saw Miss Schnee waiting with a big smile.

"Here he comes," she cooed. He looked at her with disgust. "Now don't you say a word. Just come sit down and I'll take care of everything. Oh, I can just see in your eyes that she wasn't any better, poor man."

He was seated, and she brought his Perrier. He started to open his briefcase. "Oh, no. Not after what you've been through. All work and no play . . . you know. Now I insist you eat something."

"No. Leave me alone. If you so much as speak to me again, I will have you dismissed."

"Well," she said, "I can see you at least had a good lunch."

"How can you see such a thing?"

"Your tie," she said. "I told you how much I like it, and look at what you've done. There's a stain. It looks like blood." She shook her finger at him. "I thought you weren't supposed to eat rare meat."

"Perhaps you would also like a sperm count?"

"Mr. van Golk, I know your bark is worse than your bite. You just need someone to take care of you." She dipped a napkin into his Perrier. "This will get rid of that nasty stain." She began rubbing his tie, dissolving the last of Nutti onto the napkin. "There now, it's all gone." She winked and walked to the rear of the cabin to replace his Perrier.

The flight arrived on time at seven. Achille walked slowly, almost languidly, through the corridors into passport control. He stepped to the front of a long line. "Evening, Mr. van Golk. I hope your wife is well."

"About the same, thank you."

"Sorry to hear that, sir. But at least she's holding her own."

"Yes."

"Good evening, sir."

"Good evening." Achille put his passport back into his pocket. He followed the green "nothing to declare" lights, merely waved at the agent who nodded at him, and walked through the exit, where Rudolph was waiting.

"Good evening, sir. Did you have a good trip?"

"The same," he said. "The same."

ARAGOSTA ALLA CARCIOFI

1250 grams sole
two 950-gram lobsters (females only)
125-150 grams shrimp (sword-shrimp only)

eggs	celery	tomato paste
cream	bay leaf	mushrooms
white wine	dill	white truffles
onion	butter	artichoke hearts
carrot	brandy	

Spuma
skin and bone sole. grind. beat in egg whites. beat in cream, salt, shake of cayenne. pour mousse into buttered mold. poach.

Aragosta
boil fish stock. add lobsters, simmer. cool. split. cut tail meat into slices. claw meat leave whole. season and sauté. flame with brandy.

Salsa
make lobster butter (crush lobster shells, add equal weight butter, and some tomato paste. strain). make sauce (butter, flour, salt, pepper, cream). boil sauce. reduce to simmer. add lobster butter. reserve.

Guarnizione
chop fine 125 grams white mushrooms, 4 white truffles, 125 grams shrimp. sauté. add lemon juice, salt. bind with *salsa.* fill 8 artichoke bottoms. sprinkle with sieved egg yolks.

1. Arrange *aragosta* around *spuma.*
2. Coat with *salsa.*
3. Arrange stuffed artichoke bottoms.

Serve with Soave, Orvieto, or Capri.
(for Achille, add shrimp to *spuma* and serve with a Montrachet.)

atasha sat on a sofa in the lobby of the Plaza-Athénée. Her hair was pulled back under a floppy fedora. Hidden by huge round sunglasses, her eyes were rimmed with the weariness and tension of the past days.

It was nearly midnight when she arrived. Alois, the concierge, kissed her, took her luggage, and sent a cable to Achille telling him that she was in Paris. Then Alois suggested she have a drink while he located Max. The lobby of the Plaza had always been one of her favorite places. Unlike the Ritz, one could never tell what time it was simply by looking at what the tenants were wearing. It could be noon or midnight: there would be the same overdressed Brazilians and the same exotically understated Parisians. The Plaza offered sanctuary from time.

Max sat down beside her and took hold of her hand. They looked at each other, almost without expression, neither one feeling anything need be said. It was enough to be held and to be holding. She rested her cheek against his shoulder and tears streamed from under the sunglasses. He pressed close for a moment, then helped her up. With his arm still around her, he motioned as they passed Alois for her baggage to be brought upstairs. She walked with her head resting on his shoulder. They said nothing in the elevator.

Max opened the door to his suite and led her through the living room into the bedroom. Natasha stood silently in the middle of the room while he pulled back the bedspread. He came over and took off her sunglasses. The tears were still streaming down her face. He brushed them away gently and slipped off her jacket. Natasha stared into space as he unbuttoned her blouse, unzipped her skirt and took off her underthings. She stepped out of her shoes and he slid off her stockings. The last thing Max removed was her hat. He unpinned her hair and let it fall to her shoulders. Then he helped her to the bed, and covered her lovingly.

There was a knock at the door. The porter brought Natasha's valise and alligator case into the living room. Max latched the door shut. He went into the bedroom. Natasha was staring at the ceiling. He watched her while he took off his clothes, and then he drew the drapes and turned off the lights. Once in bed, he pulled her close. She rested her head on his chest and he felt the wetness from her eyes. He stroked her hair gently. Then they became aware of his erection.

He was afraid she would misunderstand, that she would interpret his putting her to bed as a planned seduction. Ironically, he had for months been thinking how he might get her into bed. He even once thought about taking her forcibly. But not this way.

Natasha resented the hardness against her stomach. She didn't want to think about Max now; her mind was already filled with too many unformed thoughts. There was no room to consider the consequences of making love with him. It was the wrong time. Even though she felt her nipples hardening, it was the wrong time.

Max had not been embarrassed by an erection since he was in school. He closed his eyes tightly telling himself it was wrong, that he loved her too much, that this was an opportunity to show her how much he really did love her. Goddamn it, he loved her. His erection began to fade. Now what should he do? Would she think there was something wrong with him?

She felt the pressure subside, and held him more tightly. She raised her head and kissed him on the cheek. There was nothing to say.

Max woke first. Natasha was still in his arms. He got up quietly to go to the bathroom. Natasha was awake when he returned and she watched him walk toward the bed.

"I've never understood how a man could have

breakfast in bed without getting up to pee first," Max said.

"I'll unlock the door. You call room service." Natasha went to the bathroom while Max called the kitchen directly. Then she unlocked the living-room door. Max was staring at her breasts as she came back into the bedroom.

"They think I killed Louis."

"Who thinks?"

"Carmody." She got back into bed and sat upright. "Inspector Carmody of New Scotland Yard. That stupid son-of-a-bitch thinks I killed Louis."

"How do you know?"

"They told me in Rome. The police in Rome were alerted by Carmody that I was coming."

"But you're being absurd. If Carmody really thought you killed Louis, he would have held you in London. He obviously had no evidence. Besides, there was no motive."

"But then Nutti is killed while I'm in Rome."

"I still don't see there has to be any connection between the two murders except you were in both places." She looked at him angrily. "You know what I mean. And the fact they were both killed in the same style."

"That's the point, Millie. The police haven't yet picked that up as more than a coincidence. But it was no coincidence. Louis and Nutti had to have been killed by the same person, or maybe some international group of organized criminals."

"You mean like Weight Watchers?"

"I mean that someone was trying to make a statement, not merely by killing them, but by the way in which they were killed."

"So it has to be some organized group that hates food."

"Yes," she said. "Something like that."

"There's only one group that fits the description."

"Who?" she asked.

"Waiters."

She laughed and sat back. "Millie?"

"Yes?"

"Did you really cry over the silverware?"

There was a knock at the door. "Come in," Max called. The waiter rolled in a cart. *"Bonjour."* He took a folding tray from the side of the cart and set it at the foot of the bed. He put on it a small vase with a single rose, a glass of orange juice, a dish with two brioches and one croissant, butter, strawberry preserves, and coffee. "Madame," he said, giving her the tray.

He took another tray and unfolded it. He put on it a second vase with a single rose, a dish of corn flakes with a sliced banana, toast, grape jelly, and a pitcher of milk. *"Bon appétit,"* he said, and left the room.

"Aren't you ashamed of yourself?" she asked Max. "Corn flakes and bananas!"

"What should I be ashamed of? Half the world eats corn flakes and bananas. And if they didn't I couldn't afford to be in this suite now. Jesus, there you go again."

"And toast, yet. The best croissant in Paris, and you eat disgusting puffy white bread."

"Nat," he yelled, "shut up and eat."

"Now the whole hotel knows I slept with a man who eats corn flakes and bananas."

"You didn't sleep with me."

She smiled. "I know." She looked at him, reached over and took his spoon. She dipped it into the bowl and filled it with corn flakes and a piece of banana. Looking him straight in the eye, she put the corn flakes and banana into her mouth and ate them. Then she gave him back the spoon.

"That's for last night," she said affectionately.

"Old tit for tat Nat," he said bitterly. "Well, fuck you, lady. You wanna repay me for last night, you'll have to eat all of Battle Creek, Michigan." He got out of bed and went into the living room.

Natasha followed him. He was sitting naked on the cut-velvet sofa, and she stood naked in the doorway.

"You'll get pubic hairs on the furniture," she said, trying to change his mood. He sat, arms folded across his chest, staring past her. "Millie, I'm sorry. I told you I needed a friend." He stared without changing his position. "I want you to be my friend," she said.

He looked up at her. "I won't be your friend if we can't fuck."

"Conditions?" she asked.

"No. Requirements."

"What other requirements are there?"

"Exclusivity."

"Unlimited, exclusive fucking?" she asked.

"No, goddamn it. No," he yelled, and stood up. "Nat, what the hell am I supposed to do? I want you." He walked to her and held her shoulders. "I've dreamed about you for months. I've fantasized how it would be when we finally got together. Here I am, with you, in Paris, naked," he said looking down at himself, "and with another goddamn hard-on. What the hell kind of situation is this? I bring you up here, I undress you, I put you to bed, I get into bed, and I feel like a child molester. I brought you up here because I love you and I want to take care of you. I want to make love to you. But no. We sit in bed, I look at your tits, you look at my cock, we order breakfast, you tell me you want to play Nick and Nora Charles but you want me to go to the Y every night." He thrust his arms up into the air. "Do we not bleed?"

"Millie," she asked softly, "will you help me?"

"Yes," he said, putting his hands over his erection.

"Without requirements?"

"Yes."

"Then put on your panties," she said. "We have work to do."

They walked along avenue Montaigne and turned left onto the Champs Elysées. It was noon and the sun was bright, but Max was sulking. He was annoyed at Natasha's insistence on having her own room at the hotel. While she spoke to the desk clerk, Max stood behind her shaking his head "no." The clerk explained to Natasha there was not a room to be had, but he would try. Max slipped him one hundred francs not to try too hard.

"Thanks for understanding about the room," Natasha said.

"You know me," he said.

"How much did you give him?"

Max smiled for the first time. "A hundred."

"So did I," she said, pressing his hand.

"As hard as you can," he said, encouraging her to tighten her grip. "Harder."

"You son-of-a-bitch, you know that's killing you."

"You want to know what killing is?" he asked, and then pressed with all his might.

She winced and looked him straight in the eye. "Fairy." He bent over and they kissed, "Is that all I'm worth, a lousy hundred francs a night?"

"A night? That was a hundred francs for the week. If you prorate per night . . ."

"A week? I can't stay until next Friday," she said. "I'm starring at Harrods on Wednesday."

They crossed to the other side of the Champs and stopped in front of La Norma, a sprawling outdoor café. Max looked at his watch, while Natasha tried to find Auguste.

"He's not here yet," she said, sitting down at a table in front.

"They get quite a crowd here," Max said, sitting next to her.

"Why did you pick this place?"

"No particular reason. *Garçon.*" The waiter raised his hand, signaling he would be right there. "What do you want?"

"Something light. Lillet."

The waiter came over and unsmilingly said, *"Bonjour."*

"Lillet *pour madame et pour moi* Coca-Cola."

"Merci, monsieur."

Natasha shook her head. "You're not fit to take anywhere."

Max looked around at the passing parade. "This is really a terrific location."

"For what?"

"For anything. For meeting friends."

Auguste was coming toward them. A very small man, in his early seventies, his gray hair was close cropped and he wore very big steel-framed glasses. His suit was wrinkled and too large for him.

"Auguste," Max called. *"Ici!"*

Auguste spread his arms in excitement and accidentally hit a German tourist. There was a momentary scuffle during which Auguste reached into his breast pocket and took out a carving knife. Max rushed over, made excuses to the tourists, and brought a shaken Auguste to the table.

"Mon amour," he said, hugging Natasha. "It has been so long. And to see you under these conditions." There was fear in his eyes. "I have been afraid I might not live to see you again."

"But why, Auguste? Have you been sick?"

"Look at me," he said, pulling his oversized jacket away from his body. "I am like a cheap roast that is shrinking."

"Auguste," Max asked, "are you sick?"

"Sick? I have never been sick a day in my life. *Jamais.* I would be lucky if sickness were the thing I had to worry about."

"Then what is it?" Natasha asked.

"What are you worried about?" Max put his hand to Auguste's breast pocket. "Why do you carry that thing?"

"Pourquoi? Pourquoi? Because," he whispered, "of the murderer."

"The murderer?" Natasha asked, looking at Max. "What murderer?"

"What murderer?" Auguste whispered. "The murderer who murdered our dear Louis, and then murdered our beloved Nutti. The murderer who has already murdered the greatest chef in London, and then murdered the greatest chef in Rome. And what is he working toward, this murderer? It is obvious. He is next going to murder the greatest chef in Paris." Natasha and Max looked at one another, stunned by the clarity of Auguste's theory. "But," Auguste said, taking the carving knife from his pocket, "I am ready for the murderer. The murderer will never murder me."

"So, Auguste, how else have you been?" Natasha asked.

"Would you like something to drink?"

"Cognac, please."

"Garçon. Un cognac, s'il vous plaît."

"Oui."

"I am so sorry, my friends, to see you this way. In such bad times. That Nazi, I should have killed him."

"The man didn't do anything to you."

"Are you crazy? They have reoccupied Paris. It was better during the war. There were fewer of them. But enough of my problems. Tell me, I hear you have gotten married."

Natasha and Max looked at one another and laughed. "We got divorced," Natasha said.

"That was as foolish as getting married." The waiter brought their drinks. Auguste sniffed his cognac and swallowed it in one gulp. "How long will you be here, *mon éclair?*"

"Until tomorrow."

"Until Tuesday," Max corrected.

"Then I will have time to prepare a dinner for you. You will come to the restaurant Monday. At eight o'clock. Do not eat anything but an omelette for lunch." Auguste began to laugh. "I am talking about omelettes in front of him."

"You know about his plans?" Natasha asked.

"Do I know? I have been searching for him for a chef. And who do you think negotiated for him to buy this café?"

Natasha moved her heel onto the toe of Max's shoe and began pressing down. "No particular reason for being here?"

"Ouch," Max yelled, pulling his foot out from under the table.

"You do not act like you are divorced," Auguste said. "That is nice. But, *chérie,* he did not tell you perhaps because he wanted to surprise you. I think, for myself, his restaurant is disgusting. But he knows I feel this way. Still he pays me very well. So it does not matter."

"Auguste," Max asked to change the subject, "do you have any idea who might have killed Louis?"

"Of course."

"A waiter," they all said simultaneously.

"Or another chef?" Natasha asked.

"*C'est possible.* Or, if they were not so spineless, a maître."

"But who?" Natasha asked. "Do you know of someone in particular who hated Louis?"

"Everyone hated Louis. Even his friends. What does that prove? We would not kill him. His food was too good. The murderer must be someone who loved Louis, or someone who hated food."

"Auguste," Natasha began, "the police think I killed Louis and Nutti."

"*Incroyable!*"

"Do you know anyone who would have wanted to kill Nutti?" Max asked.

"Nutti is different. He was not Louis. He did not have so many who hated him."

"Do you think the same person killed Louis and Nutti?"

"*Naturellement.* And that is the reason the murderer must be a waiter or another chef. They were each prepared for cooking. I do not like to talk about it. But," he said, patting his breast pocket, "he will not get me. Have you seen Hildegarde?"

"Did the *Titanic* see the iceberg?" Natasha asked.

"You know, she knew always about you and Louis."

"I know. She told me."

"But she loves you very much," Auguste said, patting her hand.

"Thank you."

"Now I must go. They have already begun serving the lunch and I know they have ruined everything. *Ma petite,*" he said, getting up and kissing Natasha's hand, "if I am not murdered before Monday, I will see you. And you will eat a meal that van Golk himself would kill for." He turned to Max and they shook hands. "I have not yet received the check. Of course, I do not worry about such things. But you will remind them for me. After all, I could be murdered at any moment."

"I'll take care of it," Max said.

"And do not give her a hot puppy for lunch. Take her to Bertrand's. He has a new salad chef from Belgium. He talks to the lettuce. I like him very much. *Au revoir.*" He blew a kiss to Natasha, *"Mon amour."* Auguste turned briskly and walked away, holding one hand inside his jacket as though he were impersonating Napoleon Bonaparte.

"Let's go to Bertrand's," Natasha said, getting up. "Unless you've bought him too."

"No, but I've got a deal for Fauchon to package its own bubble gum."

Hiram, Hiram, Hiram . . .

You wouldn't believe it.

Somebody killed Louis Kohner. Not that he was exactly my favorite person in the kingdom, but someone knocked him on the head and stuffed him into an oven. Then they baked him. In case you want the recipe, the police say he died of suffocation because the flame took all the oxygen and what was left was hot enough to sear his lungs. Then he exploded yet. Talk about the joy of cooking. Someone had a terrific sense of humor. Oh yeah. I think I would have been the prime suspect had it not been for the lady of the evening with whom I spent the evening. Wait until I tell you what she did with marmalade. If only we could advertise it, we'd make a fortune. IT WAS BETTER THAN WHAT BRANDO DID WITH THE BUTTER!

So, being of quick wit, I xxx'd Kohner off our list and hightailed it to Paris. (Remind me to tell you what it's like to be questioned by the police. They almost had me convinced I had done it.) Anyway, you must have gotten the papers on the Norma deal. It's a honey of a place. I don't agree we should shut it down right away and keep it dark for four months. Why not let it stay open, begin moving in our staff, eggs and all, and have some practice time. Then shut down after Christmas until the renovations are finished, open in March, and be ready for the spring onslaught. Check it out. It makes more sense. They're making enough money at the Norma now to fund our trial period, which I would rather we did under their flag.

I don't like the idea of twenty types of omelettes. First of all, I can't taste the difference between American and Swiss cheese; there's hardly any difference between ham, pork, and bacon, and a green herb is a green herb. I want the following:

Omelette Naturelle (butter, eggs, salt, pepper)
Cheese Omelette (FRESH Cheddar)
Herb Omelette (fines herbes, croutons)
Spanish Omelette (tomatoes, onions, green peppers)

AND THAT SHOULD BE ALL. Otherwise we become a crêpe house. I don't want all kinds of fillings standing around getting dusty. The gimmick here should be that everything is FRESH. Fresh eggs, freshly grated cheese, fresh herbs, freshly cut tomatoes, onions, and peppers. No sauces. No frozen nothing. I want all ingredients visible. Big wheels of cheese, baskets of tomatoes, peppers, and strings of onions. I've checked prices and we can get the same price by placing a standing order for daily deliveries as we can by getting it all at once. The trucking charge is offset by our storage costs. And I think we should take the risk on serving fresh. It adds something to the tone of the place. Also, we can charge more.

The most immediate problem I see is that of the beverage. We're okay with wine, beer, coffee, tea, milk, soda, but I think we should have something unique. Not sangría, and not cider, but something we made up, and not available anywhere else. Tell the kitchen to look through their files. I like the adjective Normandy or Brittany preceding whatever the name is.

I read carefully the twelve pages on crinkle cuts vs. traditional cut and I think it's a lotta crap. Crinkle cuts remind me of Coney Island, and the others of a delicatessen. The spirals are a pain in the ass, and the onions in home fries would conflict with the omelette's taste. I say go back and try again for juliennes. With coarse salt already on them. The idea is to discourage the wanton use of ketchup, which we can do only if we give them a potato that doesn't look like their normal potato.

Also a pain in the pain is the bread crisis. No small individual loafs, no pumpernickel, no salt sticks that get soggy by the next day. The best bet, again, is the real thing. Use long loaves of French bread (have baskets filled with them also) and cut what you need as you need (knead) it. Unless the copy boys are dead set on claiming everything is done in butter (except my London marmalade lady) I think we can get away with margarine whipped into some shape. Again, don't try to make it look like butter and no one will expect it to taste like butter. But please, no butter balls. They remind me of undescended testicles. How about a fleur-de-lis mold or something?

Sheldon's designs for dishes stink. I'm pretty bored with white and green circles around the rim. Why not something really distinctive (and not the Humpty Dumpty fairy-tale pictures Sheldon tried to sell us on), like an over-all floral pattern? Something "country French" that's Busy, Busy, Busy. The real problem with Sheldon's drop-dead chic is that an all-yellow omelette with all-yellowish potatoes on a white plate does nothing for the eye. If we had a busy floral plate then the egg would stand out, and the irregular shapes of the potatoes would let some pattern peek through. Tell Sheldon to get the hell out of "dry dock country" and see how the real people live. That fag.

Jesus. I almost forgot. Dessert. I didn't like any of the ideas in Harry's report. Read it. It's ONLY FIFTY PAGES. Can you believe it? I say make it chocolate mousse, some kind of almond cookies, and maybe some (don't pee in your pants) whole, unpeeled fresh fruit. (Again, think of the display possibilities.) I'm throwing out all the reports you sent because they are shit.

I have to tell you that there's a firecracker up the ass of Paris because another chef, in Rome, was killed two days after Kohner (this one they drowned and split down the back like a lobster—I SWEAR IT ON

LAURENCE OLIVIER'S CAMERA) and everybody is watching the family jewels with great care.

Hiram, I need a few days of peace. I'm disappearing for three, four days. Trying to organize the French is like selling bagels in Cairo. Tell the powers that be I got an incurable hard-on and can't get into my pants. (Not far from the truth.)

Enclosed is a payment voucher for Auguste Foressemont. I thought I had sent it with my last letter, but forgot to. I want a check to go out TODAY, air mail special.

Don't write, wire, or call me. I fell off the edge of the earth—if only she'll have me.

Remember to comb the hair growing out of the wart on your nose.

Max

Achille opened his eyes and stared up at the ceiling fresco over his bed. He looked at them and envisioned plump marzipan bodies covered in spun sugar, ribboned with red currant jelly, holding bouquets of pastel fondant candies. The cherubs were smiling. They were constant in an ever-changing world. With Estella, without Estella, wintertime, Christmas, sickness, or spring. And even on the morning after he had killed Nutti.

He raised his hand to his stomach, rubbing slowly against his blue silk pajamas, as though trying to quell the pangs of hunger, the incessant, internal begging. That was a fine image, he thought, one with which he could compete successfully. He did not consider himself a beggar, any more than he considered himself weak-willed. He had taken the doctor's prescribed diet and given it to his staff with instructions to prepare an "edible" menu that offered no compromises. No sugar substitutes, no skimmed milk, no carrot sticks, and no fat-free cheeses. Unless he was able to eat according to the original recipe, the dish would not appear on the diet. The only concession he offered was in terms of quantity.

Indeed, the diet was tolerable because it gave him the opportunity to focus even more closely upon the quality of the ingredients and the perfection of their preparation. Even the wines, because of the limited quantity he could have, were scrutinized in an atmosphere of challenge which compensated for the small amount in his crystal goblet. In a sense, the diet was a weapon with which he could challenge the farmer, the fisherman, the greengrocer, the vintner, the chef, and God.

Although it had been nearly thirteen years since Estella last shared the bed with him, Achille continued to sleep on the left side. Once he had tried sleeping in the center, but lay awake all night. And once he had taken away her pillow, but when he got into bed he began to cry. In the thirteen years since Estella first went to the clinic, he had never had another woman. Not because he was faithful, but simply because he refused to substitute Camembert for Brie.

His hand reached almost automatically to Estella's pillow, where Cesar lay wheezing. Achille stroked the cat and he began to purr. Cesar was fifteen years old and his belly hung to the floor. White angora fur covered Cesar's legs so that when he walked, which was rare, he had the appearance of a pull toy with hidden wheels. For the past year and a half Cesar had been unable to jump and had to be lifted from floor to bed, from bed to floor. The veterinarian told Achille months ago to have Cesar put to sleep. But Achille could not bear the thought.

It was time to get up. He rolled himself to the edge of the bed, and put his feet over the side. Then he slowly pushed himself to a sitting position and, bending his knees slightly, stood up. Cesar moved as Achille walked into the kitchen. Estella had had the kitchen moved near the bedroom, since most of their meals at home had been eaten while sprawled on the bed editing articles or reading recipes to each other. He opened the stainless steel refrigerator and took out the only item it contained, a bowl of freshly boiled and cleaned shrimp. He opened a stainless steel drawer and took out a spoon of Georgian silver. He put three tablespoons of shrimp into a pink Meissen bowl. Cesar was standing on the edge of the bed meowing loudly. Achille walked back into the blue rococo bedroom and put the dish on the bed. Cesar brushed the side of his face against Achille's hand, and then began breakfast in bed.

Achille went into the pink marble bathroom. He took one pill from each of the six bottles on the shelf above the pink marble sink. He turned the gold griffin's-head faucet and filled the engraved crystal glass with cold water. After taking his pills, he reached for a small decanter and poured some cognac into the glass. He took his toothbrush, dipped it in the cognac, and brushed his teeth. He used the remaining cognac as a mouthwash.

He sat down on the pink marble toilet. After urinating and moving his bowels, he pressed a button that released a spray of hot water onto his anus. After a moment, there was a spray of warm air to dry him. Achille had the device installed because nothing was as repellent to him as the use of toilet tissue.

He walked to the doctor's scale he had recently bought. It was set at 310 pounds, his weight on Tuesday. As he stepped on it, the arm did not move. 309. 308. 307. 306. 305. He smiled with pride. Another five pounds. He had lost twelve pounds in one week. His diet was working.

After opening the stained-glass door to his shower, he unbuttoned his silk pajamas and dropped them to the floor. He turned on the shower. Water came in needle-sharp bursts from six locations, including straight up from the center of the marble floor. He used no soap, but rubbed himself with a large curved sponge. He turned off the water, stepped out of the shower without reaching for a towel, and dripped freely onto the thick mats atop the marble floor. Once at the sink he turned on the overhead heat lamp and blowers that would dry his body. With a small amount of lather from a professional hot-lather machine, he patted his face and then shaved, using a straight-edge razor with a tortoise-shell handle. When he finished shaving, he left the razor open on the sink and splashed his face and under his arms with strawberry vermouth. He walked from the bathroom without turning off the light. The policy had been adopted some time ago to leave everything for Mrs. Booth.

Mrs. Booth was once a companion to a cousin of Queen Mary. For the past twelve years, however, she had come in daily except Sunday to put back Achille's toothbrush, clean his glass, fold his razor, and pick up his pajamas. Mrs. Booth's sister, Mrs. Wickes, came once a week to clean thoroughly. Achille's flat, in addition to the pale-blue rococo bedroom, the stainless steel kitchen, and the pink marble bathroom, had an enormous living room-dining room-salon that had once been four separate rooms. One complete wall, air-conditioned behind a floor-to-ceiling glass partition, held Achille's wine cellar. Over a thousand bottles rested in vibration-free, controlled temperature behind tinted glass panels. The two parallel long walls were covered with bookcases in which resided Achille's collection of cookbooks, books about cooks, histories of food, analyses of national cuisines, and the oversized volumes in which Achille had recorded for over twenty years every meal he had eaten. On the fourth wall was an original Breughel. The room held three overstuffed sofas, half a dozen large chairs, and numerous tables and desks. The original windows in the room had been covered over to avoid the sunlight, dampness, or sudden temperature changes, which could affect the books. A constant temperature was maintained throughout the flat.

The sofas, chairs, and exposed walls were covered in a striped maroon-gold-and-blue fabric. Pale-blue oriental rugs rested on beige carpeting. Large vases were filled twice weekly with Estella's favorite flowers. In thirteen years Achille had never once sat in that room. He only walked through for a bottle of wine, or to shelve a completed volume of his dinner records. The room had once been lively with people. Friends of Estella's. Boring people, but with lovely voices.

He picked Cesar off the bed and, bending over with great care, put him on the floor. The cat brushed against his leg and then found a corner of sunlight in which to sit while he cleaned his paws. Mrs. Booth would remove the dish from the bed.

Achille sat on a high chair in order to put on his blue lisle socks. He lifted each leg slowly and with great effort. Then, holding on to the dressing-room door, he put on his freshly ironed, monogrammed blue undershorts. He took a monogrammed blue shirt from the closet and slowly got into it. He selected a maroon tie, and then his blue-and-maroon plaid suit, which felt less constricting than it had a week ago. It was nearly eleven o'clock when he left the flat and took the elevator downstairs.

Rudolph came to attention and threw his cigarette behind him as Achille walked out the front door. "Good morning, Mr. van Golk."

Achille grunted. Rudolph opened the back door and helped him inside. He picked up the morning paper as Rudolph started to drive the five blocks from his Hertford Street flat to the office on Curzon Street. He could find nothing about Nutti's death.

Rudolph helped him out of the car, and then ran ahead to open LUCULLUS's red door. "Good morning, Mr. van Golk," the receptionist said. Achille nodded. Rudolph opened the elevator doors, pressed 5, and closed the doors after Achille. As he reached the top floor, Miss Beauchamp opened the doors.

"Good morning," she said, not expecting the greeting to be returned. As they walked to his office, she stopped to pick up her notepad. It was filled with messages. She had called Achille at ten o'clock the previous evening to tell him that while he had been in Geneva, Nutti Fenegretti was killed. The chef at the British Embassy in Rome, who often translated recipes for them, had called to tell her. When Achille heard, he said merely *"Mala fortuna,"* and hung up.

She followed Achille as he sat behind his desk. For the first time, he looked directly at her. "Call the Grand. I want to speak to Natasha."

"She's not there. You got a cable this morning. She's in Paris. At the Plaza. With Mr. Ogden, no less."

"There is no less than Mr. Ogden. Call Paris, then."

"Alois had a message for her to call you. I thought perhaps I should cable her some expense money. Perhaps five hundred."

"Why did she leave Rome?"

"I don't know. I presume she was upset by Mr. Fenegretti's death. Speaking of which, Mr. Fenegretti's cousin in Manchester has called three times, and his brother in Palermo wants to be sure you're going to the funeral."

"Tell them I'm overcome with grief. Another Michelangelo has been lost. Arrange for a boys' choir to sing at the funeral. And pick up the check for whatever catering they want."

"The Les Amis de Cuisine branch in Rome wants to know if you will deliver the eulogy."

"Tell them I've been captured by gypsies, but that all their subscriptions have been extended an extra month in memoriam."

"I've written a eulogy for you. I thought we could

Telex it to Benito at the embassy and he could deliver it for you."

"Benito could not deliver the morning paper for me."

"It's being typed now. Do you want to see it?"

"Your usual diabetic prose?"

"Mrs. Kohner called. She wanted to thank you. She was the only one at Mr. Kohner's funeral. She said the boys' choir was lovely."

Achille banged his fist on the desk. "Is this a publishing house or a burial society?"

"It's an unfortunate coincidence. But these men were your friends. You can't ignore it."

"I don't wish to discuss these moribund matters any further. Deal with them as you wish. Don't involve me. I have my own problems."

"Clearly."

"Of which you are not the least annoying."

"Speaking of annoying, Mr. Tresting is most anxious to see you."

"Who is he?"

"He is the treasurer."

"The one with the heart condition?"

"Yes. He told me he hasn't seen you in six months. I explained how fortunate he was, but apparently he's self-destructive."

"What does he want?"

"He said it was confidential."

"I don't want to see him. I don't like accountants."

"He was most persistent." The telephone rang. Miss Beauchamp answered it. "Yes, he's here now, operator." She handed the receiver to Achille. "It's Paris. Miss O'Brien." He took the receiver and waved her out of the room.

"What are you doing in Paris?" he shouted into the telephone. "I had you on assignment in Rome."

"Someone murdered the assignment."

"I know. I expect to be named mortician of the year."

"Achille, within three days . . . both of them . . . what do you think is happening?"

"You must know. You were with them both."

"Achille"—her voice grew tense—"what are you saying?"

"Nothing, puss. But then again I wouldn't want you hanging around my neck as a good-luck charm."

"Achille, Inspector Carmody alerted the Rome police about me. He thinks I killed Louis."

"Rubbish."

"I know, but he thinks I did. And then I was in Rome when Nutti was killed. What do you suppose Carmody thinks now?"

"Undoubtedly he is convinced he is right. However, I do not wish to participate in your gothic fantasies."

"It's not just my fantasy. I met with Auguste. He's also convinced that the same person killed Louis and Nutti. Thank God, I've had Millie here."

"Don't tell me Flash Frozen has captured your heart again?"

"No," she said defensively. "I just need some time. A few days to recoup."

"And then what? Will you become a madam for H. Dumpty?"

"Of course not. I just need some time to think."

"An unproductive activity."

"Achille, have you seen Hildegarde?"

"No. But I understand she had a splendid time at

148

the funeral. I had the Harrow Boys Choir sing *The Trout.*"

"Achille, shouldn't I have been there?"

"Guilt is also unproductive. You seem to have cornered the market on boring symptoms."

"I shouldn't have gone to Rome. I should have stayed in London and been at the funeral. Then I wouldn't have been there when Nutti was killed."

"And now you are in Paris, missing yet another funeral!"

"I saw him. In the tank."

"Indeed."

"Achille, it was terrible. There was a lobster crawling up his arm."

"Lobsters have never been known for their manners. Listen, my love, you may comfort yourself that although you missed the funeral, you saw the murder."

"My God, you're heartless."

"Heartless? After personally insisting on an all-Schubert program for Louis? And what about the eulogy I've written for Nutti? I'm merely trying to shake you out of the heebie-jeebies, *ma fleur.* You are voraciously groveling in self-pity to the exclusion of all else. Since you did not murder Louis and Nutti, stop worrying."

"Achille," she said, becoming very serious, "you're one of the few people I really trust."

"Then take my advice. I would personally feel much better knowing you were enjoying these last few days."

"You are a dear."

"Don't snivel. After all, what are friends for?" He said good-bye, hung up the receiver, and rang for

Miss Beauchamp on the intercom. She came into his office. "I'm hungry. I want my lunch."

"It's on its way," she said. "How much weight have you lost?"

"None of your business. Twelve pounds."

"That's wonderful. You've only got a hundred and forty-three pounds to go."

There was a knock at the door. She opened it, and André, the house chef, entered carrying a tray. He wore a white jacket, black-and-gray-striped trousers, and a freshly starched toque straight up on his head. He was a wiry man with a pencil-thin black mustache.

"Bonjour, mademoiselle. Bonjour, Monsieur van Golk. Aujourd'hui le caviar avec un verre de champagne." He walked to the desk and put the tray in front of Achille. Ceremoniously, he removed the linen napkin that covered the tray. *"Voilà, le déjeuner extraordinaire."*

In the center of the tray was a richly ornamental Georgian silver bowl filled with crushed ice. A small crystal cup of caviar was embedded in the ice. André arranged the small wooden spoon and the lemon wedges so they were at right angles to Achille. He pulled back a napkin to show one slice of toast with its crust removed. Then he took the towel off the top of the ice bucket, removed a split of Bollinger '66, inserted the tulip-shaped glass upside down in the ice for a moment, opened the champagne, poured exactly four ounces, and removed the bottle and bucket. *"Bon appétit, monsieur. Bonjour, mademoiselle."* He left the room.

"What about Tresting?" she asked.

"Send him in, send him in. But *you* go away." She

left the office. Achille licked his lips. He looked at the small pearl-gray eggs. Carefully, he put his spoon to the caviar and took but a single egg. It was perfect. He pressed it against the roof of his mouth with his tongue. Then he brought the glass of champagne to his nose. He sniffed it, put his lips to the glass, and merely moistened them. He sat back thinking of how the first snowflake must have tasted to the gods on Mount Olympus. There was a knock at the door.

"Come in," he called.

Arnold Victor Tresting was fifty-six. He was a medium-sized man, with no distinguishing features. Light-brown hair, pleasant enough looking, neatly attired.

"Good afternoon, Mr. van Golk," he said, entering the room with his hand extended. Achille was busy spooning some caviar onto a small piece of toast.

"You must excuse me, Tresting, but as you can see . . ."

"Yes, of course." There was a pause.

"Well, Tresting, it must be six months at least since I've seen you. Why have you been avoiding me?"

"Oh, I haven't been avoiding you, Mr. van Golk. We've been very busy, sir."

"You are the treasurer, are you not?"

"Yes, sir."

"Then tell me, what do you treasure?"

"I beg your pardon?"

"For what treasure did I employ you to be the treasurer?"

"Well, you see, sir, I'm really more of an accountant."

"Then let us have an accounting. How do you account for the weather these days, Tresting? And how do you account for the abominable manners of the young?" He picked up his glass and again moistened his lips. "Ah, Bollinger tries, but the Dom will out."

"Mr. van Golk, I am Arnold Victor Tresting. I am the treasurer, and I have been in your employ for six months. I came to this firm after recuperating from a series of seventeen mild heart attacks." Achille looked at him and frowned. "I took this particular position because it was my evaluation the firm was showing a modest profit and no severe strain would result from my involvement in the finances of this company."

"Do you like caviar, Tresting?"

"I prefer fish sticks, myself."

"Tresting, what do you want?"

"Mr. van Golk, I merely wish to inquire whether you foresee the increasing profitability of this firm continuing at its present rate. Our subscriptions have gone up forty percent over last year, thereby increasing our profit by some sixty percent. You are becoming an exceedingly wealthy man and I am frankly . . ."

"What is it, Tresting? Trest me."

"I am frankly afraid if the spiraling profitability continues, this position will become too taxing for me. The first thing I know you will want to diversify. You will increase my wages, and both my professional and personal lives will be altered immeasurably. I have been worrying about this problem for a number of weeks and I would appreciate your assurance that you expect a decline in our profits."

Achille pushed aside his caviar. He pushed back

his chair. He stood up. "Tresting, are you seriously telling me that if this company continues to make more money it will be detrimental to your cardiac condition?"

"Yes, sir. That's it. That's precisely what I'm saying."

"Tresting, you are dismissed. Write yourself a check for one month's wages. Leave these premises within half an hour or I shall apply a magnet to your pacemaker. Do not expect you will receive any recommendation from this firm other than encompassing your suggestion you be admitted at once to Charenton Asylum. You may go."

"Yes, sir." Tresting got up from his chair, and turned curtly to leave.

"One more thing, Tresting," Achille called after him.

"What?"

"BOO!"

THE VAN GOLK DIET

Prepared by André Decharne and the staff of
LUCULLUS

1. This menu averages 1218 calories per day, allowing for the addition of reasonable amounts of coffee or lemon tea.
2. As per agreement with Mr. van Golk, he will sleep through the morning meal. There is no provision for breakfast.

WEEK ONE

	Calories per meal
Monday	

LUNCHEON

4 oz boiled lobster—103
2 T curried mayonnaise—197
4 oz champagne
  Dom Pérignon Brut '66—100   400

DINNER

4 oz lamb filet (mignonettes)—236
  each wrapped in bacon
2 slices bacon—62
2 t oil—82
2 t butter—66
4 oz leeks—59
2 T brown sauce—36
1/2 cup yellow squash—13
1 T grated parmesan cheese—27

1 4 oz peach—38
2 oz port—92

6 oz wine
  Château Mouton-Rothschild
    '49—120   831
                                    ────
                                    1231

	Calories per meal
Tuesday	

LUNCHEON

3 oz prosciutto—227	
8 oz casaba melon—62	
4 oz champagne	
Veuve Clicquot-Ponsardin Brut '59—104	393

DINNER

1 cup onion soup gratinée—92
8 oz frog's legs—166

2 T butter—200
    garlic, parsley, vinegar—trace

1/2 cup steamed carrots—27
1 T chopped walnuts—49
1 t butter—33

1 cup strawberries—53
1 oz kirsch—83

6 oz wine	
Château Laville-Haut-Brion '66—120	823
	1216

Wednesday

LUNCHEON

4 oz saumon fumé—200

*Calories
per meal*

1 slice toast—67
4 oz champagne
   Mumm Double Cordon
     Extra Sec '64—109   376

DINNER

1 cup asparagus consommé—71
4 oz roast venison au poivre—143
8 oz fresh mushroom caps—62
   sautéed in
1 T butter—100

1 cup fresh raspberries—82
3 T crème fraîche—159

6 oz wine
   La Tâche '61—180   <u>797</u>
                          1173

Thursday

LUNCHEON

4 oz roast beef—273
1 oz horseradish—11
   mixed with
4 T whipped cream—106
4 oz champagne
   Moët et Chandon Brut '61—87   477

DINNER

1 1/2 oz melted Raclette—152

8 oz poached striped bass—238

*Calories
per meal*

2 T aïoli—194
1 cup steamed cucumbers with
  fresh dill—20

8 oz Spanish melon—62
1 oz lime juice—7

6 oz wine
  Pouilly-Fumé, Ladoucette '71—120   793
                                          1270

Friday

LUNCHEON

4 oz whole grain fresh Beluga caviar—296
1 slice toast—67
4 oz champagne
  Bollinger Extra Sec '59—109   472

DINNER

1 cup jellied madrilène—60

4 oz filet mignon—245
3 T Sauce Béarnaise—156

1 small tomato grilled—24
1 t butter—33

5 fresh medium kumquats—65

6 oz wine
  Château Pétrus '61—120   703
                                       1175

	Calories per meal
Saturday	

LUNCHEON

4 oz roast pheasant—184
3 T Sauce Maltaise
   (Hollandaise and Orange)—171
4 oz champagne
   Heidsieck Monopole Brut '61—109   464

DINNER

8 oz petite marmite—40

8 oz Dover sole—180
   Sauce Amandine—240

1 cup spinach—36
1 t butter—33
1/2 oz gruyère cheese—50
1/2 T bread crumbs—13

Coffee Granitas
  1 cup espresso—0
  1 T sugar—46
   freeze, shave, serve

6 oz wine
   Wehlener Sonnenuhr Auslese
   (Joh. Jos. Prüm) '71—120   <u>758</u>
                                 1222

	Calories per meal
Sunday	

LUNCHEON

4 oz sturgeon—169
1 slice Russian black bread—57
4 oz champagne
    Taittinger Extra Sec '64—109   335

DINNER

4 oz shell steak—277
    stuffed with
4 oysters—49
2 t butter—66
2 t oil—82
1/2 oz chopped shallots—10
1 T white wine—10
2 T brown sauce—36

4 oz raw mushrooms—31
2 T lemon juice—8

1 orange—77
1/2 oz Curaçao—50
1 T freshly grated coconut—28

6 oz wine
    Chambertin-Clos de Bèze
      (Pierre Gelin) '66—180   <u>904</u>
                               1239

NOTE: It is not intended that Mr. van Golk subsist this poorly every week. We have had to estimate some of the calorie counts given above, but by next week we expect final reports from the laboratory as well as more accurate figures from the wine châteaux. Be assured that future menus will be more distinctive and varied.

atasha was awake. Max's arm lay across her chest, cupping her right breast in his hand. She watched his arm move up and down with each breath she took. Max's head was resting on an unwrinkled pillow. She smiled, remembering how she used to fight with him for sleeping so neatly. She wondered how great a commitment she had made by going to bed with him. The months without Max had been exhilarating. The bloody coup inaugurating the revolution was successful and the new government had been recognized. But now, continued isolation, or coexistence?

Unlike other men with whom she slept, Max was a

compulsive talker, telling her how he felt, explaining each sensation, requiring that she describe her feelings. He insisted that making love in silence was antisocial and selfish. Each time she moaned, he said "Tell me." After each intake of his own breath, he offered a full explanation. He wanted her to know how she pleased him, but he also wanted to know how well he was pleasing her. There was an honesty, a vulgarity, a sensitivity, and an excitement with Max she never had with anyone else. There had been others who were more romantic, but no one had ever demanded so much of her.

Yesterday, following Auguste's suggestion, they went to Bertrand's for lunch and spent hours, at Max's insistence and to Bertrand's amusement, over a cheese fondue, a beef fondue, and a chocolate fondue. They drank a white Nuits-Saint-Georges, a red Nuits-Saint-Georges, and Turkish coffee laced with Grand Marnier. Bertrand had been a waiter at the Dolder in Zurich when Max was the maître there. They were the same age and had become good friends. They shared a house and they even shared their women. Bertrand's desire for fame, to see his name in lights, was all-consuming. He overcame his middle-class waiter's morality and allowed himself to become corrupt by succumbing to a quality kitchen. Although his restaurant in Paris was a gourmet success, he was secretly writing a book on the lives of the great waiters.

Bertrand agreed with Auguste's premise that the killer would now attempt to murder the greatest chef in Paris, and, with the fervor of a true convert, proposed a survival conference with the eight chefs recognized as the best. While she and Max spent hours over their fondues, Bertrand made the phone calls. Max suggested they all meet for lunch at La Norma, but the chefs refused. In fact, they could not agree upon a single restaurant in which they would eat. Bertrand suggested they meet in the Tuileries, at noon on Saturday. Each chef would bring his own lunch.

"When I grow up," Max began slowly, "I want to be rich and wake up in the best suite at the Plaza with my hand cupped on the breast of a beautiful princess, after having spent the best night of my life." Natasha reached over and put her hand to his lips. He kissed her fingers. "Then, the beautiful princess will give me a kiss and say, 'Good morning, darling, you're the best fucker in the whole goddamn kingdom.'"

"Good morning, darling," she said, kissing him on the lips, "you're the best fucker in the whole goddamn kingdom."

Max propped himself up on his elbow and looked at her. "Do you think, when I grow up, such a thing will happen to me?"

"No, darling, I don't."

"Why not?"

"Because," she said, putting her arms around him, "there is not the slightest chance you will ever grow up. Besides, if you're the best fucker, what does that make me?"

"The best fuckee."

"Why?"

"Because The Man always fucks The Woman."

"Says who? We did it together."

"Right. But I was the fucker, and you were the fuckee. I have the thing to fuck you with."

"No, you son of a bitch. We participated equally in a joint activity. You know it was my idea to be Duncan Hines and Betty Crocker."

"Yeah," he said, "except next time *I* want to be Duncan Hines."

"What next time?" she said coolly, getting up and going into the bathroom.

Max followed her and stood outside the bathroom door. "All right. You win. But you play dirty. This is no way to begin our next divorce." He took his penis in his hand and began to shake it as he murmured, "So you're the fuckee?"

It was ten to twelve when they left the Plaza. Max complained about not having any breakfast, while Natasha pushed him along the street. They turned right at the Champs Elysées, into the Rond Point, and down the few blocks to the Place de la Concorde. It was windy, a gray day but without threat of rain.

"I should have had breakfast," Max said.

"Don't you ever stop thinking of your stomach?"

"Yes, I do. Sometimes I think about your stomach. Did I ever tell you how much I liked your stomach?"

"Darling," she said, squeezing his hand, "there's nothing you haven't told me."

"Harder," he said. She pressed his fingers tightly.

They crossed against the traffic, dodged taxis around the obelisk, and ran across to the Concorde entrance to the Tuileries. As they walked through the gate, Bertrand began waving at them. A number of people were sitting around the large circular fountain: two little boys holding a broken sailboat, a uniformed nanny with a carriage, two old women arguing, and eight silent men. None of the chefs were within speaking range of one another. They each held a small paper bag. Bertrand and Auguste walked toward them.

"I'm sorry we're late." Natasha kissed Bertrand.

"They would not sit together," Bertrand said, motioning his head to the chefs seated around the pool like numbers on a clock. "But you are here now, so perhaps they will move closer."

Auguste tugged Max's sleeve. "The check. I have not yet received it."

"You will, *mon ami*," Max said, putting his hand on Auguste's shoulder. "Trust me."

"Of course I trust you. I know you would never cheat me. An old man. I am sure it will be here Monday."

Max felt something bulky on Auguste's shoulder. "What have you got under your jacket?" Auguste smiled broadly, and as swiftly as a flasher, opened his jacket so that Max alone could see his shoulder holster and gun. "Are you serious?"

"Sacré bleu," Auguste exclaimed, clutching Max's jacket sleeve. "Do you think I want to be dead? I know. You think I will be murdered before the check comes. No, no. Not Auguste. I will be alive. I will be alive to cash the check."

Natasha and Bertrand walked away from Max and toward Henri Foullepret, who rose as they approached. "Henri," Natasha said, kissing him.

"Natasha," he said, "I am so sorry about Louis. Did he write down his *Pigeonneaux* recipe?"

She didn't know whether to laugh or get angry. Bertrand asked him to please sit with Max. Then they went to Marcel Massenet. She extended her hand, and they embraced. "Do not eat anyone else's food," he whispered in her ear. "I have made something special for you."

Pierre Legrame kissed her on both cheeks. "Where did you eat last night? I thought for certain you would come to me."

"We had *chinois*. I wanted to, but the others would have been so insulted."

"Ha! I do not know why you have asked them all here. It is clear I am the next one the killer wants."

"Please, Pierre," she said, moving him gently toward the others, "I could not bear it if anything happened to you."

"But it will," he said, without turning back.

François Vibanque sat in his chair as Natasha approached. "François," she said. He looked up.

"You are looking at a dead man. There is no way to save me."

Natasha kneeled down and kissed him on the cheek. "François, nothing must happen to you. Please, go with the others."

"Do not eat anything they have brought. I have something special for you."

Jacques Piagrette stood up and opened his arms. They embraced. He took hold of her shoulders, and shook his head. "What garbage have you been eating? How long have you been in Paris? Why have you not let me cook for you? Who knows how much time there is left? I could be killed at any moment."

"Nothing will happen, Jacques. We're all going to help each other."

He looked around at the others. "Help? From them? I would get more help from an *escargot*."

Paul Simone stood abruptly as Natasha approached. They held hands for a long moment. "First Louis. Then Nutti. And next, me. Who is doing this? Do you think it is the Russians?"

"I don't know who's doing it. It might be coincidence. We don't know for certain it was even the same person."

"But I know. In my heart, I know. And I know I am the next one. It is very clear. Where did you eat last night?"

"Chinese."

"Very diplomatic. But today, I have prepared lunch for you. Do not risk being poisoned by the others."

Roger Comise stood up and began to cry. "So this is how it ends? I have thought only of you since I heard about Louis. For myself, I do not care if I die. But you, my poor darling, you must go to funeral after funeral."

"Roger, darling. You won't be killed."

"Why not? Who deserves it more than me? Have you brought me here to insult me?"

Jean-Claude Moulineaux hugged her tearfully. "I remember the night when you and Louis and Nutti sat in my kitchen while I prepared the duck for Achille."

"We were all so drunk."

He smiled. "We laughed so hard that night. I do not know how we cooked the dinner."

"And now, you and I are the only ones left." He began sobbing.

"Please, Jean-Claude."

"I am sorry. But we are the only ones left and who knows which one of us will be next?"

Natasha stood frozen as Jean-Claude turned away. His words "which one of *us* will be next" rang in her ears. Until that moment, she had been merely a suspect. Jean-Claude had suddenly changed her role to that of victim.

Max had arranged the chairs in a circle. Natasha sat down next to him and held on to his arm. She leaned over and whispered, "Big M, I think I'm going to die."

"You should have eaten breakfast," Max whispered.

"No. I mean really going to die. Jean-Claude thinks I'm on the hit parade."

"Jean-Claude is a frog-frying fag, not Ellery Queen." Max turned to the group with a smile. "Well, you may wonder why I've asked you all here." No one smiled back. "Yes," he continued seriously, "we're here to see if you have any idea who's responsible for what's happened."

The chefs looked at one another. They raised their eyebrows, shrugged their shoulders, and shook their heads.

"I have already told you," Auguste shouted, getting up from his chair. "It is a waiter."

There was a murmur of disapproval from the others. "There is no waiter smart enough," Henri said.

"There are some smart enough not to work for you," said Roger.

"Waiters do not have money to go from London to Rome to Paris."

"They have more money than you think."

"That's right. From what they steal."

Bertrand got up angrily. "I was a waiter. I did not steal. And I was smart."

"You were smart enough to stop being a waiter."

"But you were stupid enough to open your own restaurant."

"So now they steal from you."

"You call that a restaurant?"

"If he is so smart, why does he overcook his carrots?"

"How would you know if I overcook my carrots? You have never eaten my food."

"I sent my cousin."

"Who would have killed Nutti?" Max asked. "Do you have any ideas?"

"If he was killed like a lobster, then perhaps someone did not like the fact that Nutti killed lobsters."

"What kind of maniac would that be?"

"A vegetarian?"

"Perhaps Jacques Cousteau?"

"Does your cousin like lobster?"

"It's a shame you will not be next."

"You think you will?"

"Ask your cousin."

"Please," Natasha began, "two of your friends have been murdered. There is the possibility the killer may try to murder one of you." Then she slowly corrected herself. "One of us."

"Not one of me," Max said to her. "I can't even boil a pizza."

"Maybe he will not kill a French chef next," Roger said.

"Maybe he will kill a Swiss chef."

"Maybe," Natasha whispered to Max, "he will kill an American chef."

"Then let's cable Colonel Sanders."

She pinched his arm. "Louis, Nutti, Jean-Claude, and I once cooked dinner together."

"Which one of you got pregnant?"

"Two of them are dead," she said.

"I always knew you were a lousy cook," Max answered.

"Maybe Klaus Hoerbner?" Paul asked.

"Klaus Hoerbner died two years ago," Pierre reported.

"No!"

"I was at the funeral. They served petits fours."

"I want to know why the killer did not kill a French chef first. In all due respect to Louis and Nutti, if someone is killing chefs, you should certainly first kill a French chef."

"That is true."

"It is a national insult."

"It proves the killer is crazy."

"Or he is very clever. He is leaving the French chef for the last. I see it all. He is building to a crescendo."

"What do you know?"

"I know I do not freeze my veal."

There was shocked silence. Roger stood up. "Are you accusing me, here, in front of everyone, of freezing my veal?"

Henri stood up, facing Roger. *"Mais oui."*

Roger pointed his finger at Henri. "There is your killer."

"Roger, please," Natasha said.

"I demand an apology," Roger yelled. "He is lying. He is lying. I do not freeze my veal."

"One of my waiters said he does."

Everyone shrugged and told Roger to forget about it. It was obviously a lie if it came from the mouth of a waiter.

"I will never forgive you for this," Roger said.

Henri sat down. "I will try to live without your forgiveness."

"I am beginning to think this whole meeting was a mistake," Bertrand said. "You cannot think of anything but pettiness. You cannot even stop bickering long enough to have thoughts of the danger you are in. Well, if you do not care, I do not care."

"He's right," Max said. "Let's try to think of some clue as to who the killer might be."

Marcel got up and gave Natasha his bag. "This is for you. I have made it specially."

Francois came over. "This is better. You will eat my lunch instead."

One by one they came to Natasha, giving her their lunches.

"Thank you," she said. "I'll take them back to the hotel with me."

"But how will you know which is mine?" Marcel asked.

"It will be the one that makes her sick," Francois said.

Jean-Claude stood up. "Louis is dead. Nutti is dead. I do not want to die. I do not care about your cousin, or your veal, or your carrots. If there is not something we can do, then I wish to leave." He sat down. Everyone was quiet.

"I think we should tell the police."

"Tell them what? That we each think we will be killed by someone we don't know for a reason we don't know? The police will not help us."

"Then let us have our own police. We know when the killer strikes. The murders have taken place in kitchens when the chefs are alone."

"You see," Max whispered to Natasha, "you don't even fit the pattern. No kitchen. No alone. Besides, we have to wait."

"For what?"

"To see who gets murdered next. If it's anyone but Jean-Claude, you're safe. If it's Jean-Claude, we'll begin to worry."

"And what the hell do I do in the meantime?"

"In the meantime, I've decided to donate all my semen to helping you forget."

"Millie, you goddamn fool, what if I'm killed before Jean-Claude?"

He thought a minute. "I don't know," he whispered. "Then I guess I'll donate it to a sperm bank."

Bertrand stood up. "We have a plan."

"I will get a bodyguard."

"I will get my cousin."

"I will bring my dog."

"The dog will steal your recipes."

"He would know enough not to eat your food."

"Gentlemen," Max said. "I think we've made some progress. Go back to your kitchens, but be sure you're never left alone. Keep someone with you at all times. Tomorrow is Sunday. All your kitchens will be closed."

"Not mine," Pierre said. "The hotel kitchen is open and I am working."

"You have nothing to worry about. I do not even know how you got invited to this meeting."

"Pierre," Natasha said, "just keep someone with you."

"It is me!" Pierre yelled. "It is me he is after. You see how it fits in place? I am the only one who will be working tomorrow."

"Then we will all have dinner at your restaurant tomorrow and die with you."

Natasha took the bags and stood up. "My friends, be careful. Please. And thank you for these. I will know who has made each one. But now you must excuse me. I am not feeling well." She walked around the circle to kiss them good-bye. They each leaned over to whisper in her ear.

"Mine is the *pâté*."

"Mine is the *pâté*."

"Mine is the *pâté*."

"Mine is the *pâté*."

"Mine is the *pâté*."

"Mine is the *pâté*."

"Mine is the *pâté*."

"Mine is the *pâté*."

Dearest Mami:

Years ago, when I was alone and frightened, you took me into your home and into your heart. I need you again. I am alone and frightened again.

I am also ashamed to be writing this letter after you said you didn't want to hear from me. But there is something I must tell you while there is still time.

When I asked you to come with me, I thought I wanted to help you. But I wanted you to help me. I thought I was the stronger of the two, but you were. You didn't need me as much as I needed you.

I'm frightened, Mami, because I'm suddenly aware that life is not a forever thing. And I feel so guilty because I've wasted time that never belonged to me. I keep wondering if Louis would have done the same things if he had known how little time was left. I don't think he would have. He would have been with you, not with me. If he were to have lived forever, he might have allowed the time with me. Perhaps.

Louis never loved anyone but you, Mami. That's true. As true as the fact that no one ever loved Louis but you. You were the only person strong enough and gentle enough to love him. I think you know that.

I'm writing this, Mami, because I love you dearly. I am so very sorry for the hurt I've caused you.

Tasha

ayfair was still asleep as Achille left his flat and walked into the empty street. It was eight-fifteen Sunday morning. It was cool. Sunny. A very pleasant lemon sun. A pleasant enough day on which to kill Jean-Claude.

He knew he would never find a taxi cruising. He would have to walk to Park Lane. No matter. No doubt the entire day would be filled with distasteful chores, not the least of which was the necessity for him to establish his alibi. He thought, as he turned the corner and walked to an empty taxi, that murder indeed had its negative aspects.

"Good morning, sir." The red-faced driver smiled at Achille.

"Take me to Victoria Station. With dispatch!"

"Victoria? Twenty past eight. And with dispatch?" the driver repeated, nodding his head, and then turned around to smile again. "I guess it's going to be the eight-forty-five to Brighton."

"Incredible!" Achille said in genuine awe. "How could you tell such a thing?" he asked with a sudden tinge of fear.

"I ain't been driving for forty years, thank you very much, with my eyes shut. Now the question is, why would a gent like yourself be going down to Brighton so early on a Sunday?"

"Surely you must know that as well."

The driver laughed without turning around. "You've got a way with words," he said. "Might be an actor. But I've never seen you," he said looking back to study Achille, "and I never forget a face."

Achille smiled broadly. Then he began to laugh.

"Well," the driver said, "I can tell you this much, you weren't laughing when you got in. Your mood has changed considerable. Must be, begging your pardon very much, that you're going down for something you don't like."

"How cunning of you," Achille said archly. "Indeed, how right you are. I am on my way to making a call of condolence."

The driver formed his lips into a circle and inhaled loudly. "Ooooh, then excuse me very much, you certainly have my sympathies."

"A dear friend of mine was baked."

"Did you say *baked?*"

"I said, a dear friend of mine was baked."

"You said a dear friend of yours was baked."

"Scotland Yard say his stomach exploded."

Another sharp intake of breath. "Exploded?"

"Yes. I found that rather unexpected." There was a long pause. The driver narrowed his eyes involuntarily, aware that his palms were sweating. Achille, to his own great surprise, wanted very much to continue. "He died, actually, when the heat seared his lungs. Then his stomach exploded while his skin began to burn." Achille was thrown forward slightly as the taxi came to an abrupt halt. "What's wrong? Why have you stopped?"

"Begging your pardon, I don't feel very well." The driver leaned his head against the window.

"I'll miss my train," Achille yelled. "Get on with it. Start driving. I mustn't miss my train."

"If you'll excuse me, I need a minute. I'll get you there, but you'll have to wait a minute. Forty years I been driving." A moment later the taxi began to move.

"Coincidentally, after my dear friend from Brighton was baked, another dear friend was drowned in a lobster tank and then split down his back."

"God Almighty!"

"In a sense," Achille mused.

"Baked? Then split? Sounds like someone was getting ready to eat them."

"You should have seen . . ." Achille stopped suddenly.

"Seen what?" the driver asked.

"Your face. You should have seen your own face."

"Well, begging your pardon very much, I ain't

179

never heard of people being carved up for supper."

Achille smiled. "The last supper," he said, thinking it for the first time.

When they reached Victoria Station, Achille gave the driver a five-pound note. "My name is Achille van Golk. I live on Hertford Street. Thank you for sharing my uncontrollable grief."

Achille went to the ticket window and rapped sharply on the glass. The ticket clerk was reading his newspaper. "I doubt you are paid to read your newspaper rather than service the public."

"I'd be happy to service you," he said flatly and put down his paper.

"I wish to purchase a first-class round-trip ticket to Brighton. I will be leaving on the eight-forty-five and returning today on the two-forty-five."

"It don't matter to me when you come and go. I'm not your personal confidential secretary."

"Indeed! And what is your name? I intend to report you for rudeness and a slovenly appearance."

"You want a ticket or you don't want a ticket?"

"Of course I want my ticket. I must have my ticket in order to get to Brighton on the eight-forty-five and return today on the two-forty-five. How much is it?" Achille handed the clerk a one-hundred-pound note. The clerk stared at it for a moment and then looked at Achille without speaking or moving. "Well?" Achille asked.

"Who in hell are you kidding?"

Achille took back his hundred-pound note and replaced it with a five-pound note. "No one cares about the problems of the privileged these days."

The clerk took a ticket, and then wrote something on a piece of paper. "Here you are, your lordship. Track 9. Your ticket, your change, and my name and number for you to report me. A very good day to you," he said, smirking, and returned to his paper.

"You have not heard the last of Achille van Golk!" Achille turned and walked into the station. He looked at the clock. It was eight-forty. He passed waiting rooms filled with old men and old women with no place to go. He walked carefully around people as though they were contaminated.

Upon reaching the first-class cars, he selected one that was empty. He waited until the conductor shouted "All aboard." When it was clear he would have the compartment to himself, he opened the door and stepped up into the train. Achille smiled as he folded the piece of paper with the ticket clerk's name and put it into his wallet. He looked out the window as the train left Victoria Station. He sat back. It would take six minutes to reach Clapham Junction. While he waited, he took a large amount of change from his trouser pocket and put it into his jacket pocket.

At the Clapham station, Achille got off, made his way quickly through the station and over to a bank of pay telephones. He walked into one of the red booths and closed the door behind him. He picked up the receiver and dialed "0."

"May I help you?"

"I wish to call Paris, France. The number is Odéon 6185."

"Station to station, sir?"

"Yes."

"That will be twenty-eight pence for the first minute." Achille began dropping in coins. "Thank you, sir. I'm ringing." He heard the phone ring. Once. Twice. Three times.

"Oui?"

"Jean-Claude, are you alone?"

"Oui. Yes. Who is this?"

"This is Achille."

"Mon Dieu. I have been thinking all night about you."

"And I about you, my dear friend. Jean-Claude, I am on my way to Paris. I must see you at noon today."

"Today. *Merveilleux.* But is something wrong, my dear friend?"

"Jean-Claude, I am depending upon you. You must not tell anyone you have spoken with me. Or that you are meeting me."

"But why? Natasha will want to see you and . . ."

"No! Jean-Claude, my dear friend, it is urgent that no one knows I am coming. It is Natasha I must see you about. I'm afraid there is distressing evidence that points to Natasha as the killer."

"But no, I do not believe . . ."

"Listen to me. I have no time to argue. I am trying to save your life. No one must know you are meeting me."

"Of course, my dear friend. Come to my house."

"No."

"The Louvre? We will meet at the Louvre."

"No. I must be alone with you, my dear friend. The restaurant is closed today?"

"Oui."

"Then I will meet you there. In the kitchen."

"But . . ."

"But what? Jean-Claude, this is a matter of life and death."

"Of course. I will be there. I will leave the door open for you. Achille, I am very frightened."

"Do not worry, dear friend. I promise to put an end to your fears."

"May God bless you, my dear friend."

"At noon," Achille said.

"Au revoir, mon ami."

Achille hung up the receiver. He took another coin from his pocket and dialed.

"Bonjour. Air France."

"I wish to confirm my flight," Achille said. "I will fly to Paris today on the ten-thirty and return this afternoon on the one-forty-five."

"Thank you, sir. I'll check that. What is your name, please?"

"Thomas," he said. "Hardy Thomas."

Upon arrival at Orly, Hardy Thomas went through immigration and customs and then stepped out of the terminal to hail a cab. *"Tour Eiffel, s'il vous plaît."*

"Merci."

Achille reached into his pocket for his French franc notes. He sat back and thought of how hungry he was. At the Eiffel Tower, he got out of the taxi, paid, and waited for the driver to pull away. Then he hailed another cab to Place de la Madeleine. He looked at his watch. It was five minutes past twelve.

After waiting for the second cab to pull away, he

crossed over to the rue Tronchet. When he reached the blue canopy of Le Canard Sauvage, he glanced around to see if anyone was watching. He put his gloved hand on the service door, turned the knob, and entered. He locked the door from the inside. Jean-Claude, hearing someone, ran into the hallway.

"Thank God it is you. They told us not to be alone in the kitchen and here I am sitting alone with the door open. I am so relieved you are here. I was afraid to be late, so I have been here early. I have plucked the feathers from six ducks already waiting for you."

"I am sorry."

"Achille, is it true? What you said about Natasha? I cannot believe it. How do you know?"

"I have friends at Scotland Yard."

"*Mon Dieu.* I cannot believe it. I was talking to her only yesterday about the night she and Louis and Nutti were sitting here while I made for you my brilliant pressed duck."

"I remember," he said, looking around at the pans. "You know, Jean-Claude, your *caneton* is my very favorite."

"Thank you, Achille, I know. I wish I could make it for you now. Would you like that? While we talk, I could make it for you."

"No. There is not enough time. Besides, I am on a diet."

"But that is impossible. How can *you* live without eating?"

184

"I have been told that all the food I have eaten is killing me."

"Mon Dieu." He dropped the duck he was holding. "What is the world coming to?" he asked as he bent down to pick it up.

Achille took a frying pan and, stepping behind Jean-Claude, raised his arms and hit him on the head. Jean-Claude screamed as he fell to the floor. Achille stepped back and took off his jacket. He put on a white coat so that his shirt would be covered, and then tied an apron around his waist to shield his trousers. He took a heavy steel mallet and bent over Jean-Claude. With two blows from the mallet he crushed Jean-Claude's skull. He moved away quickly so that his shoes would not be touched by the spreading pool of blood on the floor. The huge chrome duck press that Jean-Claude had designed to hold up to four ducks sat on top of a butcher-block table. Achille put both his arms under the duck press and lowered it to the floor. Slowly he began pushing the duck press across the floor to where Jean-Claude lay. He turned the wheel so that the steel cover would be raised as high as possible. Breathing heavily, he bent down to place Jean-Claude's head into the bucket of the duck press. He became nauseated at the sight of splintered skull, hair matted with blood, and the exposed pinkish-gray brain. When he had the body propped against the duck press, and the head in position, he began to turn the wheel so that the flat steel disk would press down on Jean-Claude's battered head. Once the disk reached the face, Achille had to turn with great force. He could hear the cracking of bone and then saw the slow outpouring of Jean-Claude's blood from the spout. Finally, Achille could turn the wheel no more.

He took off his apron, folded it carefully, and placed it on the table. Then he took off the white jacket. Still careful not to get his footprints in the blood, he walked to the stove, turned it on, and set the jacket and apron on fire. He dropped them into the sink, where they continued to burn. He turned on the water to douse the flames. Then he took off his gloves and put on his jacket. He put one glove in his pocket, and put the other on to shut off the water. He stepped around the body, turned off the light, and walked to the door. With the glove on his hand, he unlocked the door, put the safety latch on, and after poking his head out to be sure no one was watching, stepped out of the doorway and walked down the street toward Boulevard Haussmann.

At the corner he stepped into a phone booth. *"Mademoiselle, donnez-moi London, England, s'il vous plaît. Je voudrais trois sept cinq vingt-neuf, trente-neuf."*

"Quel est votre numéro?" she asked.

"Vingt-deux, treize."

"Très bien, merci."

Achille waited a moment, readying his change. He deposited the coins immediately after she requested them.

"Hello?" Rudolph asked.

"I don't care what you're doing. I have taken ill on

my way to Brighton. I will rest awhile and arrive back at Victoria Station at three-forty-five. Bring the car. Meet me without fail." He hung up before Rudolph could answer.

Achille stepped off the curb and hailed a taxi. *"Orly, s'il vous plaît."*

CANETON À LA PRESSE "LUCULLUS"

1 Rouen duckling (6 weeks old, from Yvetot only.
Buy from Gaspar or Figo. Notify 2 weeks ahead for
special feeding. Can be up to 8 weeks old if special
fed.)
Kill by asphyxiation. Do not lose any blood. Save
liver.
Stuff duckling with *mousseline*:
Sauté chopped onion in 125 gr. chopped bacon fat. Do
not let onions color. Add 3 duck livers, 125 gr.
chopped mushrooms, 2 truffles, 100 gr. *foie gras,* 50
gr. boiled chestnuts, chopped parsley, one lump of
sugar, mace, salt, pepper. Sauté. Add red wine. Cool.
Pound in mortar. Rub through sieve.

1. Roast stuffed duckling for 18–20 minutes. Carve
   in thin slices. Remove legs, make incisions, season with salt, pepper, pounded clove. Grill legs.
2. Chop duckling liver. Cook with port and cognac
   over high heat.
3. Remove *mousseline* mixture from duckling and
   place in center of platter.
4. Crush carcass in duck press, collect all blood.
   Add *consommé* from carcass of another duckling,
   then add to liver mixture. Beat until thick. Warm
   duckling slices in sauce. Arrange on platter.
   Pour remaining sauce over slices.

Serve with *pommes soufflées en nids*.
Serve legs with the *salade*.
Serve only with a Chambertin.

When the telephone rang on Monday morning, they were asleep at the foot of the bed. Max crawled over Natasha and picked up the receiver. "What time is it?" he asked.

"Jean-Claude has been murdered." It was Bertrand.

Max leaned back against the headboard. "Jesus."

Natasha sat up and faced Max. He avoided her eyes as Bertrand continued. "It was the worst of them all. His head was crushed in the duck press. He was found this morning. It must have happened yesterday. The police will come to you soon."

"The duck press," Max repeated, looking at Natasha for the first time.

"I am sorry, but I thought you should know right away."

"Terrific." Max hung up the receiver. Natasha was sitting bolt upright, her breasts heaving with each breath. Max cleared his throat. "We'd better get dressed," he said calmly. "I think I'll wear my camel's hair. Why don't you put on something incredibly inappropriate?"

Her eyes filled with tears. "Ask not for whom the *quenelle* tolls," she said softly.

They met in the living room and sat down on the sofa, like guests at a cocktail party.

"Did you know her well?" she asked Max.

"Know who?"

"Natasha. Natasha O'Brien Ogden O'Brien. The darling departed."

"Did Jekyll know Hyde?"

"Aside from her tits," she asked, "what did you like best about her?"

Max looked at her seriously. "I loved her because she never said die."

"That's not the story I heard. I heard she finally gave up."

He took hold of her hand. "Darling, I've never seen you like this."

"Darling, I've never been murdered before."

"You're not going to be murdered," he said angrily. "I'm too young to be a widower. Ex-husband is as far as I'm willing to go."

"Millie, I'm the only one of the four of us left. Louis, Nutti, Jean-Claude, and I each made one course that night. They were each killed in the order of the courses. I made the dessert."

"The *Bombe Richelieu*?"

She shook her head yes. "I'm next on the menu." He turned away from her. He knew it was the truth.

"Well, maybe not," he said after a moment.

"Why not?" she asked, anxiously leaning toward him. "For God's sake, tell me why not!"

"Maybe the killer doesn't want dessert. Maybe he's on a diet."

Natasha and Max rode in separate squad cars at the insistence of the police. The cars raced through the morning streets, their hiccupping sirens reassuring citizens that the Republic had caught its prey. When they reached the Sûreté, a paddy wagon was being filled with prisoners. Natasha and Max held each other's hands. They walked inside with two policemen in front and two behind.

"When I was arrested in London, there was none of this fanfare," Max said.

"When I was arrested in Rome they didn't even take me to the station house." Natasha pressed his fingers tightly.

"Actually, I think this is one of your classier arrests. It's the snazzy uniforms."

"I'll bet the holsters are from Dior." They were led into a small waiting room. There was a worn oak bench, two straight-backed wooden chairs, and a standing ashtray that was overfilled with cigarette butts. "*Maison et Jardin* all the way," Natasha said, sitting down.

Inspector Griege, a slight, very short man of about five feet, with an unruly head of frizzled gray hair, was smiling at them from the doorway. "I have catched you in the act," he said. Natasha stood up immediately. "I am the Inspector Griege." He walked toward them and extended his arm. "I wish to congratulate you on the unfortunate death of Monsieur Moulineaux," he said sincerely.

"Congratulate?" Max asked, shaking his head.

"That is not the right word? I wish to express my *congratulations?*" Then he slapped his forehead with the palm of his hand. "Oh, no, no, no. I wish to express my *condolences.* You must forgive me. My English is wonderful. Please, come inside and let us sing together."

They followed him into his office, a room filled with shelves of old books, pictures of Buffalo Bill Cody and Chief Sitting Bull. There was a pair of crossed tomahawks on one wall, and a large brown-and-white cowhide skin on the floor. Inspector Griege's desk set was made out of the same spotted cowhide.

"How do you hate this?" he asked, raising his arms and pointing to the walls and furnishings.

"It's just wonderful, Inspector," Max said. "Makes me feel right at home."

"It is lovely," Natasha offered.

"Thank you. Thank you." He pressed the buzzer on his desk. Two men entered the room. "Now I have made you feel good, I must ask that you each go into a less room so that we may drink your statement. Miss O'Brien, you will go with Monsieur Contron, and Mr. Ogden will go with Monsieur Suplice."

Natasha and Max looked at one another, and then at the two narrow-eyed young men. They rose and were each ushered into a separate small room that had only a table and two chairs.

"May I see your passport, Miss O'Brien?"

"Yes, of course."

"You were not born in America?"

"No. I'm a naturalized citizen."

"How long had you known Mr. Moulineaux?"

"Mr. Ogden, can you tell me where you were on Sunday?"

"We slept late, left the hotel, and went for a walk along the Seine. We took a boat ride. We had lunch at a café on the Left Bank. We went to the Eiffel Tower. We walked along the Champs and had dinner at La Norma, then we went back to the hotel."

"You and Miss O'Brien?"

"Yes."

"You were together all day?"

"All day and all night."

"I see."

"Were you more than friends with Mr. Moulineaux?"

"He was a dear friend," Natasha said.

"Did you have a romantic relationship with him?"

"No."

"You were married to Mr. Ogden?"

"Yes."

"And now you are divorced?"

"Yes."

"But you are staying together at the same hotel?"

"Yes."

"Do you have now a romantic relationship with him?"

"It's hardly romantic, but if you're asking whether we sleep together, yes."

"I see."

"But Mr. Ogden, how could you be so certain that another chef would be killed?"

"We weren't certain. We were just trying to protect them."

"So then you would know exactly where they were all of the time?"

"Yes. No," Max corrected as he understood the implication. "So that we would know they were protected."

"But the protection did not work."

"No. It didn't."

"Perhaps because the killer knew he had to strike before the chefs were protected in their kitchens."

"Yes. Maybe."

"Because the killer knew that on Sunday the chefs would not be guarded."

"Perhaps."

"Perhaps? It seems very clear. It would indeed be clever to win the confidence of the chefs by offering them a plan and then kill before the plan goes into operation."

"Just what are you implying?"

"Only that it would have been a clever thing to do."

"So you were with Mr. Ogden the entire day?"

"Yes."

"Did anyone see you?"

"I would presume so."

"People who could swear they saw you?"

"I don't know. We were at La Norma."

"What time was that?"

"Around six."

"After the murder. Who saw you earlier?"

"I don't know. Isn't it enough that Mr. Ogden saw me?"

"You were married. You were divorced. You are sleeping together. You are each other's alibi. It is like the wife testifying for the husband."

"But we're not married any longer."

"A technicality. But I do not think a jury would believe such alibis."

"A jury?"

"Is it true that you tried to hire Mr. Moulineaux for your restaurant?"

"How did you know that?" Max asked.

"Would you please answer?"

"Yes. I did."

"And what was his reply?"

"That he would sooner die."

"He did not like your restaurant?"

"No. He did not."

"And you were upset with him?"

"Auguste told you that I had an argument with Jean-Claude." The policeman was silent. "Yes. We argued. I told him that I thought he was a pompous ass. Like the rest of them."

"The rest of them?"

"The other chefs who didn't want to work for me."

"So there were other chefs who rejected your offer?"

"Yes."

"And you do not think very highly of them?"

"I don't see what that has to do with anything."

"Please answer the question."

"No. I don't think very highly of them."

"But you called a meeting to try to save their lives?"

"Yes."

"Even though you did not think highly of them, and some of them had rejected your offers?"

"Yes."

"This new restaurant is very important to you?"

"Yes."

"You are working very hard to ensure its success."

"Yes."

"But you have not been able to find a chef who would work for you?"

"I will."

"But you have not yet found one."

"No."

"This could not please your company very much."

"They know I will find someone."

"But you are surely under great pressure."

"Miss O'Brien, you are a feminist?"

"I am a person."

"But you believe that women have been repressed by men?"

"Yes."

"You believe that women should have the same pay as men?"

"Yes."

"You believe that women should have the same opportunities and jobs as men?"

"Yes."

"They should be chefs, as men are."

"Yes."

"Why?"

"Because women can do the same things that men can. There is no difference between a man or a woman in the kitchen."

"But it is surely very hard work?"

"Yes. But we're not butterflies."

"You think that women can do all the same hard work in the kitchens as men?"

"They've been doing it at home for centuries. Why not get paid for it?"

"They can handle the same tensions? The same equipment?"

"Yes, of course."

"The same duck press?"

"And what did you do when Miss O'Brien told you she thought she might be killed next?"

"I told her not to worry."

"But you were worried?"

"Yes."

"Did you tell Mr. Moulineaux that you were afraid he might be killed?"

"That was the reason we had the meeting. We thought one of them might be killed."

"But she told you of her conversation with Mr. Moulineaux and of her fears. What did you do then?"

"I ordered dinner and we watched television."

"Did this chef in London who was killed also refuse to work for you?"

"No."

"Did you ask him?"

"No."

"Was he not a good chef?"

"Yes, he was."

"Then why did you not ask him?"

"I didn't want to."

"But there must be a reason."

"It was a personal reason."

"May I know the reason, please?"

"It has nothing to do with anything." The police-man looked at Max, waiting for an answer. "I did not like him."

"Why?"

"He was sleeping with Miss O'Brien."

"You were in London when he was killed?"

"Yes."

"So you were in London when that chef was killed, and you were in Paris when Mr. Moulineaux was killed."

"If you think you are to be killed, why did you not come to the police?"

"Because . . . what would you have done?"

"You began to say 'because.'"

"Because I was questioned in the other murders."

"And you had enough of the police?"

"Yes."

"But since you were not guilty of the other murders, why would you not do everything possible to save your own life?"

"I couldn't be certain that my own life was really in danger until Jean-Claude was killed."

"And so you were waiting for him to die?"

"No. I wasn't *waiting*."

"You were in London and in Rome when the other chefs were murdered?"

"Yes."

"And now you are in Paris when Mr. Moulineaux is murdered."

"Yes. Yes, yes, yes. But I didn't kill him."

"Because you were on the Eiffel Tower?"

"Yes."

"And in Rome?"

"I was at the Forum."

"You do a great deal of sightseeing."

"Of course, you may call a lawyer. But I do not think it is necessary. I am only trying to understand where you have been. You have not yet been charged with anything."

"Yet?" Max asked. "Listen, there is a lady next door who is going to be killed unless you stop wasting time and find out who the hell is carving everybody up."

"You are sure she will be next."

"Yes."

"How do you know? I mean, since you are not planning it, how do you know for certain that she will be next?"

"How do you know for certain that *you* will be next?"

"Because the killer has followed the pattern of a dinner. Hors d'oeuvre, fish course, entrée, and next is dessert."

"And you are the dessert?"

"Yes."

"You mean someone is committing murder according to a menu?"

"Yes."

"And by coincidence you have been in each city that each chef was killed in and by coincidence you are the dessert. So now after they are all dead, all men whose jobs any woman could have done, now after they are all dead you come to us and say that you need protection against this menu killer?"

"What are you trying to say?"

"I am only trying to understand."

"I think you're trying to understand too damn much. I've told you where I was yesterday. If you don't believe me, prove that I was somewhere else. If you have proof, then charge me and I'll get a lawyer. If you have any further questions related to my whereabouts when Jean-Claude was killed, ask them. Otherwise, I don't intend to answer any other questions."

"But I am sure you have nothing to hide."

"And I'm sure that I don't have to put up with your insinuations. I need your help, not your suspicions. But I can damn well do without both." Natasha got up and walked out of the room. Inspector Griege was seated at his desk aiming a Colt .45 at the opposite wall.

"Ah," he said, quickly shoving the gun into his drawer, "I did not expect you would have been begun so soon."

"Inspector, I need your protection."

"But, Monsieur Contron will not harm you."

"Inspector, someone is trying to kill me."

"But no. You are very safe here. This is the Sûreté."

Natasha turned as she heard Max's voice yelling, "Don't you understand, someone is going to kill her!" It was the first time she had heard her terror verbalized by someone else. Suddenly it all seemed too real. She was telling the police someone was going to kill her. Max was telling the police someone was going to kill her.

The door to Max's room opened, and the other policeman came out. He went to Inspector Griege and they spoke very quietly for a moment. "Monsieur Ogden, if you would be good as to come in here." The three men left the room.

Natasha and Max sat down. They looked at one another and said simultaneously, "They think I did it," and began to laugh. Then Natasha began to cry.

"Listen to me," Max said. "Each murder has taken place when the chef was in the kitchen alone with the killer. That's the pattern. That's how the killer works. We know that. All we have to do is keep you out of the kitchen, or be sure someone is with you."

"But that's what we told Jean-Claude. That's what we told everyone. We knew that."

"Then we also know Jean-Claude went to the kitchen because he thought he was safe. The killer had to be someone Jean-Claude knew and trusted."

"And that's what they're saying, Millie. They know Jean-Claude knew and trusted us."

"Well, make up your mind, damn it. Are you more worried about being the killer or the killee?"

Inspector Griege came back into the room.

"Inspector, Miss O'Brien needs protection. She will be in Paris for another two days."

"She is going away?"

202

"Yes. She has to be in London on Wednesday. You have no reason to detain her."

"I do not have any at this hour. But I would like her to stay upside down for a few days more in Paris."

"You can't keep her here."

Griege walked back to Suplice and shrugged his shoulders. They argued for a moment and then Griege came back to Max. "You are both free to went after you give us each a separate statement."

"But what about protection? I want her to have police protection while she is in Paris."

"But of course I will protect her. I think *she* is the killer!"

"I've already heard," Achille said.

"From who?" Max asked. He put his hand over the receiver and whispered to Natasha, "He doesn't miss a murder!"

"Auguste told me," Achille said. "He called and reversed the charges. He said he had no money because you hadn't paid him."

"Son of a bitch."

"How is Natasha?"

"Couldn't be better. She's convinced she'll be murdered next."

"And knowing you, you've been feeding this paranoia of hers."

"I will bring her to London tomorrow. After the funeral. I want you to hire a bodyguard for her."

"Of course. I'll have the bodyguard at the airport. Just deliver her to London and I'll take care of the rest. Let me speak to her."

Max sighed. "The beneficent Oz himself." He gave the receiver to Natasha.

"Achille, darling, I'm terrified."

"Listen to me and do not speak. You are with a hysteric. Remember that he with whom you share your bed requires noises from his morning cereal. What he requires from you is none of my business insofar as it does not affect your work. Kindly bear in mind you are expected at Harrods on Wednesday. Until then you would do well to stop flattering yourself that someone wishes to kill you."

"I suppose that's meant to be reassuring."

"Have I ever neglected you?"

"No, Achille, you never have."

"Then be reassured. I shall take very special care of you in London."

STATEMENT OF INVESTIGATING OFFICER

Case No. 87765/Moulineaux   17/9   Suplice

Subject: Maximilian Ogden
Attachments: Taped interview (16/9)
                    Signed statement (16/9)
Comment of Investigating Officer:
   Subject is in the process of opening an omelette restaurant in Paris on behalf of a large American food processor. According to the taped interview, the deceased refused to work for Ogden because he thought the project unworthy. It is possible that Og-

den, under great pressure, killed Moulineaux in anger. He could have convinced his ex-wife, with whom he is now having an affair, to provide him with an alibi which, although a weak one, gives him more on his side than we have against him. Or, he could be threatening her in some manner.

I am concerned with the London and Rome murders, although they are beyond our jurisdiction. I know we cannot use suspicions in those cases to strengthen our own suspicions but I believe we are dealing with a situation of multiple murders. I believe it is possible

1. Ogden killed the London cook because
   a. he was having an affair with his ex-wife,
   b. he rejected Ogden's business enterprise.
2. Ogden killed the Rome cook because
   a. he was going to have an affair with his ex-wife,
   b. he rejected Ogden's business enterprise.

Although we cannot yet prove Ogden was in Rome at the time of the murder, we know how simple it is to get a forged passport, and that would be no problem for someone with money.

We have here an interesting mix of sexual competition and professional rejection. It is my opinion that a man as dynamic and attractive as Ogden, with an insecure personal life and pressures from a large corporation, could respond in a criminal manner.

Recommended action: Continue surveillance.

STATEMENT OF INVESTIGATING OFFICER

Case No. 87765/Moulineaux   17/9   Contron

Subject: Natasha O'Brien
Attachments: Taped interview (16/9)
              Signed statement (16/9)
Comment of Investigating Officer:

I find this case very confusing. Based upon the facts, the subject was with her ex-husband at the time of the murder. There is no apparent motive for her to have murdered the deceased. Indeed, she has expressed her fear that she may be a potential victim. While there is no way to prove she was *not* at the scene of the crime (except the questionable testimony of her ex-husband, who could be an accomplice), we also cannot prove she *was* there. On just these facts, there is no substantial reason to consider her a prime suspect.

However, there have been two other murders where her alibis (I have read the reports forwarded by the London and Rome police) are even weaker. I realize that our jurisdiction is limited to the Moulineaux murder only, and on that alone we have no motive to assign to her, but this would appear to be a case of multiple murders for which the solution or motive may be found (as we have seen in other such cases) at the scene of one of the other crimes. If we consider our impressions as in a multiple murder case, and not merely on the killing of a chef on the rue Tronchet, then:

1. She was in the other cities at the times of the other murders;

2. She is a women's liberationist who must clearly resent the men in her profession;

3. She knew all of the victims. There is possibly a sexual motive aside from the feminist angle: a) she was having an affair with the London chef (Kohner), who was her stepfather (Guilt); b) she was to begin an affair with the Rome chef (Fenegretti), who also had been a long-time "family friend" (Resentment at being used as an object of sex—and perhaps guilt at wanting to begin an affair so soon after Kohner's death); c) she knew that Moulineaux was a homosexual and had no interest in her (Anger at being sexually rejected, and anger that the "false" gender of Moulineaux allowed him status in a profession in which she fought for recognition).

On the basis of these points, I would consider her a prime suspect. However, the subject's "menu" theory that she is the next victim is not without reason. I cannot dismiss it as merely a ploy to throw us off her track. There is as much logic in the argument that she may be the next victim as there is valid suspicion that she may be the killer.

Recommended action: Maintain surveillance of subject.

RECORD OF TELEX

Mode: Top Priority
To: D. I. Carmody
New Scotland Yard/London

From: A. C. Griege

CANNOT HOLD OBRIEN FOR MOULINEAUX MURDER STOP
URGE REPEAT URGE YOU PLACE HER UNDER TIGHT SECU-
RITY WHEN SHE ARRIVES IN LONDON STOP BELIEVE SHE IS
NOT REPEAT NOT KILLER OF CHEFS BUT THAT SHE IS NEXT
TO BE MURDERED

The Place de la Madeleine was, as always, filled with cars. On this Tuesday, double-parked in front of the entrance to the church was the black hearse that had brought the body of Jean-Claude Moulineaux. Inspector Griege arrived early and was seated inside. Contron and Suplice were across the street watching as the bereaved walked up the steps to the entrance. They saw Natasha and Max leave their taxi. Flammiste, who had been assigned to follow them, promptly pulled up in his car. Once Max saw that Flammiste had parked, he led Natasha into the vestibule.

Bertrand walked over to them. "The sun is shining, but it is a sad day. I am surprised you have come."

"We're safe," Max said. "We're being followed by the gendarmes."

"Is Jean-Claude's sister here?" Natasha asked.

Bertrand shrugged. "I did not know he had any family."

"He had a sister," she said. "I met her once. She was much older than Jean-Claude. She had wanted him to be an engineer."

"Why an engineer?" Max asked.

"It is obvious," Bertrand said. "Engineers live longer than chefs."

"Bonjour." It was Auguste.

"Good morning," Natasha said.

"I do not speak to the crook here," Auguste said, pointing at Max.

"The check will come, Auguste."

"And they will discover truffles on top of Sacre Coeur?"

"Please," Nastasha said. "Not now. Not here."

"You are right," Auguste said. "It was a terrible accident."

"Accident?" Max asked.

"Of course. You do not expect me to believe that the murderer meant to kill Jean-Claude. No, it was an accident. The murderer will realize his mistake and look for me. But I am prepared." Auguste opened his jacket to show his gun and shoulder holster. Suddenly two men lunged at Auguste and knocked him down. Max grabbed hold of Natasha and pushed her away.

"Au secours! Au secours!" Auguste cried. Max and

Bertrand tried to stop the two men but were pushed aside.

"Police, police," Bertrand yelled.

"We are the police!" one of the men screamed. They had Auguste stand with his palms against a wall as they frisked him and took away his gun. Inspector Griege came from inside the chapel.

"And so we have closed the shirt on another case!" he announced proudly.

Bertrand explained that the police had made an error, but Auguste was arrested for carrying a gun without a permit. As they took him away, Auguste shouted at Max, "You will stop at nothing to avoid paying me!"

Natasha put her arm in Max's. "Millie, let's go inside." They walked down the aisle and saw Inspector Griege fingering a small lasso in the back row. The seats were filled with chefs and waiters momentarily united by a common grief. Natasha and Max stood in front of the altar.

Atop the polished mahogany casket was Jean-Claude's toque. It stood straight like a giant white mushroom. At the insistence of Jean-Claude's sister there were no flowers. She had requested instead that donations be made for the purchase of new drafting equipment for the Sorbonne's School of Civil Engineering. Arranged on easels around the casket were photographs of the dishes Jean-Claude had created, a blowup of his review in the *Guide Michelin,* and a gold-framed photograph of him presenting a leg of lamb to Charles de Gaulle. There was also a picture of Jean-Claude, Louis, Nutti, and Natasha with their arms linked. Natasha could not take her eyes from the photograph. Max tried to lead her to a seat, but she stood fast, staring at the picture.

"I don't think you remember me. I am Jean-Claude's sister."

Natasha looked down at the old woman who stood next to her. "Jean-Claude was a very dear friend. I am so sorry. We will all miss him very much."

"*Oui*. And now he will never become an engineer."

"You should be very proud of him. He was a very good man, well respected."

"You think he was? I always thought of him as strange. Always cooking little cakes in the kitchen. It was not natural. He never married. But, what woman would marry a man who makes little cakes in the kitchen?" She began to cry. "I told him, 'Build *la Tour Eiffel, le Pont-Neuf,* even the *Autoroute.*' But all he did was to bake little cakes."

Max tried again to pull Natasha away. She held his arm tightly and refused to move. She refused to take her eyes from the picture of Louis, Nutti, Jean-Claude, and herself. Not since she was a child during the war had she felt this smothering sense of impending doom.

A choir of fifty boys dressed in white robes appeared from the sides of the altar. The choirmaster stepped forward and sat down at the organ. Max led Natasha into a pew. The choir began to sing *My Heart Is But a Lamb*. Natasha whispered to Max, "Do you think the killer is here?"

"I hope so. He deserves to suffer like the rest of us."

A prayer was offered by the priest. Then the chef from the British Embassy stood in the pulpit to read a tribute by Achille.

"An artist has died before the canvas was finished. Those of us who cherished his friendship, and his food, will forever be hungry. For the rest of our lives, there will be a portion of our appetites that cannot be sated. But our memories are rich, and we shall have to sup from them."

There was a murmur of appreciation.

"It's Achille!" she whispered to Max.

"Where is he?"

"No. Don't you see? Each of the chefs cooked part of Achille's favorite dinner. Don't you understand? It's got to be Achille!"

"Are you serious?"

"Yes! It's Achille he's after! The killer is someone who hates Achille."

Bertrand rose from his seat and walked to the pulpit. He put his papers down, and cleared his throat. "What is the measure of a man such as Jean-Claude? I will tell you. One cup of happiness, one cup of charm, two cups of sensitivity, a teaspoon of . . ."

"Millie, the killer is someone who hates Achille enough to murder Louis, Nutti, Jean-Claude, and me. He's trying to stop Achille from ever again having his favorite dinner." They knew that was it. They knew who the killer was. The only thing they didn't know was his name.

"Season liberally," Bertrand continued, "for he loved the spice of life. . . ."

At the close of the service, Jean-Claude's sister walked up the aisle behind the casket. Then, without speaking a word, each chef nodded at the others, walked down the steps, and went in a different direction. Natasha and Max stopped at the corner, waiting for Flammiste to start his car. Inspector Griege offered them a police escort back to the hotel but they declined. Instead, they walked a few blocks, each trying to think of who hated Achille enough to kill the chefs.

"It's like trying to find a piece of hay in a haystack," Max said. He looked behind him for a moment as they walked. "It's okay. The *flic* is on our tail."

"Thank God, they think I'm the killer. Millie, I want to call Achille and warn him."

"Warn him of what?"

"That someone hates him. That he's in danger."

"From what? Why would the killer knock off Achille? If you're right, Achille is the last person to be killed. The purpose of the murders is to make Achille's life miserable. Someone hates him too much to kill him."

"But shouldn't he know? Maybe he could help us find out who it is."

"Nat, do you know how many people hate Achille?"

"I know. I'm scared, Millie."

"You're perfectly safe. Nicholas and Alexandra should have had such protection. There's nothing to be worried about. We have Flammiste and his flying Citroën, Sheriff Griege and his posse, and, most of all, you have me and my magic penis."

"No offense, but I'm still not renewing my subscription to *TV Guide*."

He stopped to face her. They heard the screech of brakes as Flammiste's car came to an abrupt halt. "Listen, babe. You'd be crazy not to be scared. But there's a pattern to the murders. Unless you're alone in a kitchen somewhere, you're safe."

They continued walking. "The killer must know I'm aware of that. He's got to be planning something different for me."

"All right. All right, I confess." Max stopped and spread his arms out. Flammiste's brakes could be heard. "I intend to love you to death."

She smiled. "Am I supposed to say 'what a way to go'?"

"Marry me, Nat."

"I did marry you."

"You never married me in Paris. Let's become each other's beneficiaries again."

"What a rotten way to make a buck."

He laughed. "I love you."

"Everybody loves an endangered species."

He smiled and put his arms around her as they turned the corner into the rue Cambon. He stopped before going into the back entrance of the Ritz to be sure Flammiste had seen them. They went into the art deco bar, and sat on the corner banquette. Two very old women, with almost as many jewels as jowls, sat smoking cigarettes and drinking their Martinis straight up. Across the room sat a tall, white-haired man with a slender blond boy who spoke animatedly with his hands. They also drank Martinis straight up. Max ordered two Margaritas and began to eat the peanuts. In the mirror behind the bar, he saw Flammiste's reflection. Max turned around. "Hey, you want a drink?" he called. But the moment he spoke, Flammiste disappeared into the corridor. "Just trying to be friendly," he muttered.

The waiter brought the drinks. Natasha and Max picked up their glasses and clinked them. "To Jean-Claude," she said softly. *"Adieu."* They emptied their glasses in one gulp. They looked at one another while they were still holding the empty glasses, and nodded. Simultaneously they smashed their glasses on the edge of the table. Everyone in the bar froze. Flammiste ran into the room. Max acknowledged each look with a smile, and when the waiter came over, handed him fifty francs. He ordered another round and assured the waiter there would be no toasting. They sat silently while the waiter cleaned the table and brushed the glass from the floor. "Millie, there's something I think you should know."

"What?"

"I don't want to die just because someone hates Achille. It's pretty ego deflating. I want to be murdered on my own merits."

The waiter brought another round. "*S'il vous plaît, monsieur,*" he implored as he put them on the table.

"Poor Achille," she said. Then she began to laugh. "My God, if murder weren't permanent, it would all be so funny. Who would kill Louis, Nutti, Jean-Claude . . . and me because he hates Achille?"

"I can't imagine. Who could hate Attila the Honey?"

"Millie?"

"Yes?"

"If someone baked Louis because Achille's favorite dish that Louis made was a baked pâté . . ."

"Nat!"

"And someone split Nutti like a lobster, and someone put dear Jean-Claude in a duck press . . ."

"Then you want to know . . ."

"Tell me, darling, do you think I'll be beaten or frozen?"

"I'd opt for frozen. Saves wear and tear on your clothes."

"I could even be whipped."

"A little SM *mit Schlag*. Whipped cream and chains. Not bad."

"Oh, Millie."

"I know." He put his arm around her.

"Millie," she began thoughtfully, "I'm beginning to feel that dying isn't all it's cracked up to be. Besides, I know how he's going to do it."

"How?"

"Simple." And then she whispered, "He's scaring me to death."

Flammiste was sitting in a chair, reading a newspaper, when they came out of the bar. Max walked over and pulled the paper from in front of his face. Flammiste stood up automatically. "Hi," Max said. "We're leaving now and going back to the Plaza. How about giving us a lift?"

Flammiste was flustered. He nodded his head yes. They followed him to his car. He opened the back door and they got in. "I mean there's no need not to be civilized about it," Max explained as Flammiste began to drive. "Besides, I've wanted to congratulate you on the fine job you've been doing." Flammiste looked at him in the rearview mirror and smiled awkwardly.

"However," Natasha began, "as they say, all good things must come to an end. Watch the car in front of you, he's making a left! We're leaving Paris this afternoon for London." Flammiste turned quickly to look at them in his mirror. "I know, darling. I hate good-byes, too."

"Not that it hasn't been fun," Max said. "But we thought we'd tell you now so that you could contact X-12 without having to rush. Careful, that bus is pulling out in front of you!"

"Say, why don't we all go to the airport together?" Natasha asked.

"Sure," Max said. "It's got to be a schlepp for you to keep following our taxi—watch out for that Mercedes!—so why don't we make it easy on everyone's nerves."

Flammiste looked back again. "Make a left at the next corner, darling. Think about it," Natasha said as they drove up to the Plaza. Flammiste opened the back door and helped them out. He followed them into the lobby.

Max and Natasha walked to the elevator, waved good-bye to Flammiste, and went up to their suite. Once inside, Natasha locked the door and began taking off her clothes. By the time she reached the bed, she was naked. She lay down and held her arms out to Max, who was struggling out of his shorts, having flung his clothes all over the floor.

"Last tango in Paris?" she asked.

Ever since leaving Paris, they had felt completely vulnerable. Natasha and Max sat close, walked close, and averted their eyes from all but each other. Once through British immigration and customs, they were met by Achille's chauffeur. Behind him was a young man with the thick neck, enormous shoulders, and barrel chest of a comic-strip character. He wore sunglasses with metallic-coated lenses. His eyes were not visible.

Max nodded at him, and he nodded back. Natasha whispered to Max, "He has no eyes."

"He doesn't need eyes. He's got teeth."

"I'm scared."

"Of him?"

"Of the thought of him. Of needing him."

"You weren't scared of Flammiste."

"He was like a friend."

"So make a friend."

Natasha turned toward him and extended her hand. "I'm sure you know who I am. How nice to meet you. What's your name?"

"Lucino," he said thickly, without offering his hand.

"Hi, Lucino," Max said brightly. "We're the good guys."

"I guard only her."

"Right," Max said. "Good Lucino," he muttered as they walked out of the terminal and over to Achille's black Phantom. Rudolph opened the door. Achille was smiling.

"At last! The return of Pineapple Poll!"

Natasha sat next to him and took hold of his arm with both her hands. "I'm so happy to see you."

"Of course you are. After the company you've been keeping, an attack by red ants would be soothing." He patted her hand. "You look absolutely dreadful. It must be all that freeze-dried sex," he said, watching Max pull down a jump seat and face him.

Max smiled. "Hi, sweetie!"

"Achille, I've been so frightened."

"Do remember this is the land of the stiff upper lip."

"Still Mister Softee," Max said.

"Millie, please let's not bicker. I'm so very tired, Achille. You're one of the few people I can trust."

Rudolph and Lucino seated themselves up front. The car began its journey to London. Max nodded his head toward Lucino and asked quietly, "Where did you get him?"

"I sent the labels from my caviar jars and half a crown to the NKVD."

"Achille," she began, "the reason I think I'm going to be killed has something to do with you."

"Splendid. I've felt so left out of all this."

"Achille, there are some things only your best friends will tell you," Max said.

"Do not flatter yourself."

She began gently. "We believe Louis, Nutti, and Jean-Claude were killed because someone hates you."

"Indeed. And was I also the cause of the Franco-Prussian War?"

"Listen to me, darling. They each made one course of your favorite dinner. They were killed in the order of the courses. And they were killed as though they were part of the recipes for those dishes."

"And you fancy yourself the dessert?"

"Yes."

Achille began to laugh. "It's absurd. It's the most absurd thing I've ever heard."

"Achille, I'm terrified!"

"Terror is part of life, my dear. It does not give one a license for lunacy. You cannot seriously expect me to believe that anyone could possibly hate me."

"It might come as a surprise to you, Achille, but perhaps on an off-day you alienated a few thousand people." Max shrugged his shoulders.

"Natasha, my darling, was it not I who wanted to open a charlotte russe factory in Bangladesh?"

"Achille . . ."

"Did not I suggest sending round-the-clock *quiche* when the coal mine collapsed in Wales?"

"Achille, don't . . ."

"And . . ."

"Achille," she yelled, "someone hates *you* enough to kill *me!*"

There was a pause. "Do you think *I* might be in danger from this madman as well?"

"No," Max said. "That's the kicker. I don't think you're in any danger at all. The murderer thinks he's hurting you more by killing off your favorite chefs."

"To whom have you told this incredible theory?"

"To no one," Natasha said. "I didn't want to get involved with the police again. But there's no more time, Achille. Someone is planning to kill me, and you're the only person who can help."

"You have only to ask, puss."

Max leaned forward. "Achille, I think you know who the killer is. You may not know he is a killer, but you *know* him. Now, I grant it could take a lifetime to investigate everyone who hates you, but there must be a few standouts in your mind."

"Can you think of anyone, Achille?" Natasha clutched his arm. "Do you have any ideas at all? If you could think of someone, you might save my life!"

Achille sat silent as Natasha and Max looked at him. "Well, I congratulate you both. I cannot recall another time I have been at such a loss for words."

"We need you, Achille. You've got to give us some names." Max waited for an answer.

"I cannot think of anyone who would wish to harm me." Natasha and Max sat back in exasperation. "However, I shall reconsider the possibility."

"Darling, I'm running out of time. You've got to think fast."

"Natasha, I promise to think of who among my legion of dear friends is trying to kill you. In the meantime, you will never walk alone. You will have either me or Max at your side. I presume Peter Plastic will share your chamber this evening."

"Yes, but I have to go back to Paris in the morning," Max said.

"No matter. Lucino and I will escort you to Harrods tomorrow, where you will be surrounded by an adoring throng."

"I think we should go to the police anyway," Max said.

"No, Millie, I won't go through that again. The police can't do anything. I won't be subjected to their endless questions, their innuendos . . . I just can't."

"Of course you can't," Achille said, soothingly. "Surely, Max, she's already been through enough without further mindless prodding. Really, I don't see the harm in a day or two in which to recoup."

"She might not have a day or two, that's why."

"Stop referring to me in the third person! I'm still alive."

"That's what I'm trying to guarantee."

"Millie, Achille is right. Give me at least a day or two. I won't be alone. If Achille comes up with something, we'll go right to the police. Otherwise, I'm not ready to go through the agony of convincing Carmody I'm not the killer but that I'm going to be the victim."

"One day," Max said. "On Thursday morning I go to the police."

"Agreed," Achille said. "On Thursday morning we shall meet with the police and present my list of suspected assassins."

"Millie, it's okay," she said, taking his hand. "Nothing can happen to me tomorrow."

Achille darling,
Here it is. Now do be careful. Isn't this fun?

As ever.

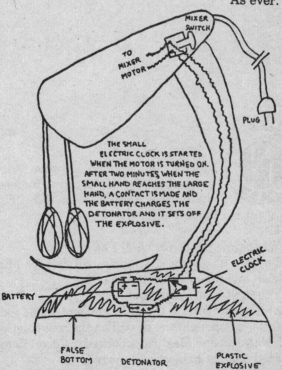

THE SMALL ELECTRIC CLOCK IS STARTED WHEN THE MOTOR IS TURNED ON. AFTER TWO MINUTES WHEN THE SMALL HAND REACHES THE LARGE HAND, A CONTACT IS MADE AND THE BATTERY CHARGES THE DETONATOR AND IT SETS OFF THE EXPLOSIVE.

MIXER SWITCH

TO MIXER MOTOR

PLUG

ELECTRIC CLOCK

BATTERY

FALSE BOTTOM

DETONATOR

PLASTIC EXPLOSIVE

atasha, Max, and Lucino were dropped at the Dorchester. Rudolph then drove Achille to his flat. "Will you want me this evening, sir?"

"No."

"What time tomorrow shall I be here?"

"Be here at eleven sharp. We will call for Miss O'Brien and take her to Harrods."

"Thank you, sir. Good night, sir."

Achille walked into the building, and, as he rode upstairs, his thoughts were still on the conversation with Natasha and Max. He unlocked the door. Cesar brushed against his foot and purred.

Achille sat down on a chair in the foyer. He felt his heart pounding and was suddenly aware that his body was covered with perspiration. He leaned over to pat Cesar. After a moment, he stood up and removed his clothes, leaving them in a pile on the floor. He walked naked into the bedroom and turned on the Chopin sonata tape. Cesar meowed loudly until he was fed the chopped lobster Mrs. Booth had left in the refrigerator.

Achille stepped into the shower. He allowed the water to wash away the perspiration and then stood under the heat lamp while the blowers dried his body. A few splashes of strawberry vermouth across his chest, on his forehead, under his arms, and then he put on his blue silk robe. He walked through the living room and opened the door to the wine wall. Behind the shelves, among the cases, was an unmarked square carton. He carried the carton into the kitchen and lifted it onto the stainless steel counter.

He was perspiring again. For some reason, it had never occurred to him they would think he held the key to the murders. But what if they did? There was no evidence that he was involved. They could suspect whatever they wanted. There was simply No Evidence. He went back into the living room, to the bookshelves. From inside his copy of *Les Misérables* he took the passport of Hugo Victor. From within *The Return of the Native* he took Hardy Thomas' passport. And from behind his set of *The Story of Civilization* he took the small brown envelope that contained C3, a plastic explosive.

Once in the kitchen, he placed the C3 envelope atop the square carton. He lit one of the burners on the stove and set Hugo Victor and Hardy Thomas aflame. He put them into the sink to burn. That was the end of his only connection with the Rome and Paris murders. He used a paper towel to clean away the ashes in the sink and flushed them down the toilet.

Achille untied the twine and took off the wrapping paper. The carton itself was imprinted with a likeness of the new Hansen electric mixer that Les Amis de Cuisine had formally approved. He opened it carefully so that it could be resealed. He extracted the gleaming white mixer and its steel beaters from the polyfoam mold. He stared at it. Using a small screwdriver, he took off the false bottom that had been built into the mixer. From behind the picture of a Spanish melon above the counter, he untaped the drawing of the mixer and detonating device. He studied the drawing, almost unwilling to believe it could be so simple. He opened the C3 envelope, took out what appeared to be a package of semisoft clay, and proceeded to pack it into the base of the mixer. Then he screwed the base back and burned the diagram. With great care he wiped all his fingerprints from the mixer, put it back into its polyfoam mold and then into the carton, which closed with a series of interlocking tabs. He fit the wrapping paper back around the carton, sealed it with tape, and retied it with the twine.

Using a thick black marker, and writing with his left hand, he slowly printed in block letters

HARRODS

URGENT PRIORITY FOR MR. ST. CLAIR

SPECIAL EQUIPMENT FOR BBC COOKING DEMONSTRATION

THIS EQUIPMENT IS TO REPLACE MIXER

IN EXHIBIT KITCHEN

FRAGILE   FRAGILE   FRAGILE

THIS SIDE UP   THIS SIDE UP

Achille put the carton and the black marker into a large paper carrying bag. The Chopin was still playing as he began to dress. It was dark outside. Cesar glanced up for a moment as Achille closed the door.

Once in the street, Achille walked quickly, carrying the bag close to the building. After two blocks, he hailed a taxi to Piccadilly Circus. The driver stopped at Piccadilly and Lower Regent Street. Achille walked down the stairs to the Underground, made his way through the labyrinth of corridors, and found a secluded area where he rented a locker. He took the carton out of the bag, pushed it to the back of the locker and secured the door. On his way out of the station, he threw the bag into a litter basket. He walked back up the stairs into the neon frenzy of Piccadilly Circus at night.

Suddenly he wanted to be part of the crowd. He wanted to nod at pleasant-looking ladies. He watched slender young men as they jousted with each other and wanted to tell them how daring he had just been. But then, after only a moment, he wanted to go home, to be closer to Estella.

At nine o'clock the next morning, Achille was freshly shaved and showered. He wore a tan raincoat with a white silk scarf knotted at the neck. He left his flat and walked to Park Lane, where there was a public telephone booth.

"Harrods. Good morning."

"Mr. St. Clair, please."

"Thank you."

"Mr. St. Clair's office. Good morning."

Achille cleared his throat and raised his voice to the level of a dowager empress. "Good morning. BBC here. May I please speak to Mr. St. Clair about the cooking demonstration?"

"One moment, please."

"St. Clair, here. May I help you?"

"This is Miss Gompers. BBC. I'm afraid there's rather a sticky problem concerning the demonstration with the American chef this afternoon."

"What do you mean? We've had adverts in the papers for days. I'm expecting an overflow crowd."

"Mr. St. Clair, I'm afraid you haven't confirmed receipt of the special equipment. Our messenger service delivered a special mixer and we haven't received your confirmation that you replaced the old mixer with the new one we sent to you."

"What are you talking about? I've received no mixer. I have no notes here that any equipment was to be expected. Now see here, we've put quite a bit into this demonstration and I don't want your messengers mucking it up."

"Mr. St. Clair, I suggest you contact your receiving room at once. They undoubtedly have the parcel in question. I'll ring you back to be sure you have it. You know how these Americans are. You can't imagine what we've had to put up with here. Ta for now."

Achille stepped out of the booth and hailed a taxi. "Piccadilly Circus, please."

He walked down into Piccadilly Station, went directly to his locker, and opened it. He glanced about quickly, took off his scarf and raincoat, and put them into the locker. Achille was wearing a faded blue coverall. He took a crushed blue cap from his pocket and put it on his head. Then he took the carton from the locker and closed the door. He walked to the nearest phone booth.

"Harrods. Good morning."

"Mr. St. Clair, please."

"Thank you."

"Mr. St. Clair's office. Good morning."

"Miss Gompers. BBC. Has your Mr. St. Clair located the missing mixer?"

"Oh, Miss Gompers. I can't tell you the rage Mr. St. Clair is in. You know this whole demonstration was his own idea, having the same dessert served to Her Majesty re-created by the cook who made it at the Palace. He's beside himself."

"I should think that's the last place he would want to be. Unless he's found that mixer, I'm certain the American will refuse to cook. I surely will be forced to bring back our camera crew."

"Oh, I know he'll find it. He's gone down to the receiving department himself. You can imagine how upset he is, if he did that. But are you sure it was sent yesterday?"

"My dear, we at the BBC tell Big Ben the correct time! Surely, we can manage a wee parcel. I trust your Mr. St. Clair fares well."

"Oh, I'm sure there'll be no problem, Miss Gompers."

"There had better not be. Else heads will roll."

Achille hung up, walked quickly to the ticket booth, and said "Knightsbridge." He got his ticket and walked through the gates following the blue signs for the Piccadilly Line. As he arrived on the platform, a train was just pulling in. He stepped in and sat down. He looked around, thinking the people were truly not much worse than those who ride the airlines. Green Park Station. It was all rather an interesting interlude, apart from the mingling of undeodorized passengers with overly deodorized trains. If only people realized the importance of the sense of smell. Hyde Park Corner. Animals realized it. But at some point, as man became less a predator, he allowed his nose to atrophy in favor of his tongue. Another folly of the middle class. Knightsbridge.

Achille walked out of the station and onto the crowded street. He put on a pair of large sunglasses that would hide his eyebrows. Turning left, he crossed to the Basil Street side of Harrods and into the large open delivery area. No one took notice of him as he walked to the edge of the receiving platform. Mr. St. Clair was screaming at the men and blaming their stupidity for the fall of the British Empire, devaluation, and the energy crisis. Achille put the package onto a moving conveyor belt and walked quickly across the street.

The conveyor belt carried the package almost into the hands of St. Clair, who put the carton under his arm and stormed out of the receiving room. The men made obscene gestures with their hands as St. Clair slammed the door behind him.

Achille walked back to the Knightsbridge Station. He took the Underground to Piccadilly Circus and went to his locker. He removed his cap and sunglasses, put the scarf around his neck and then got into his raincoat. He walked up the stairs, hailed a taxi, and went back to his flat.

It was ten minutes to ten. Cesar looked up from the floor, where he had fallen asleep next to his half-eaten dish of lobster. Achille took off his blue cover-all and hid it in the back of the closet. He picked up the telephone.

"Harrods. Good morning."

"Mr. St. Clair, please."

"Thank you."

"Mr. St. Clair's office. Good morning."

"Well, have you found it yet?"

"Miss Gompers? Yes. He did. I'll let you speak to Mr. St. Clair."

"St. Clair here."

"Well, St. Clair, have we a show today or have we not?"

"Indeed we do. I myself have the parcel. However, I was personally in the receiving room when it was delivered this very morning. Not yesterday. And so it appears that the BBC is not as infallible as one might be led to believe. Eh?"

"Mr. St. Clair, to err is but human, as they say. I'm jolly well relieved that you now have the package, and the envelope with the special instructions."

"What envelope?"

"Let's not joke about at this point, St. Clair."

"What envelope?" he repeated. "There was no envelope. Just a carton with lettering all over it as though it were written by a mental deficient. This side up. Fragile. Fragile. Fragile. Et cetera. But I assure you there was no envelope."

"But I personally told them to affix it to the outside of the package. Perhaps you should see if the envelope is inside."

"Very well. Just a moment." Achille heard the receiver being put down and the shrill voices of St. Clair and his secretary as they searched for the envelope. "No. Damn it. See here, Miss Gompers, you had better tell me what was in that envelope. I don't want to have to report you to your superiors."

"I certainly hope you won't do that, Mr. St. Clair."

"Only if I must."

"I can tell you what the instructions were. I typed them myself. I know what they are."

"Then would you mind telling me?" he said angrily.

"It appears that the beaters have been preset and positioned at precisely the correct angle. The American appears somewhat paranoid about this. I can't tell you what she put us through. Well, I suppose if you've cooked for the Queen . . ."

"Will you please give me the instructions?"

"Mr. St. Clair, the simplest thing is to carry the mixer gently to the exhibition kitchen. Have one of your workmen remove the mixer you already have there. Put this mixer down. Be very careful not to jostle it, lest the beaters come out of alignment. Plug it in. Turn it on for the slightest fraction of a second, just to be certain the current is working. Then leave it alone. Don't allow anyone but Miss O'Brien to touch it. She's threatened to walk off the stage if the mixer isn't exactly the way she wants it. So I would suggest, unless you want an auditorium filled with very angry lady shoppers, you do exactly as I've said."

"Is that all?"

"Yes. But I warn you she's a terror. It seems the beaters rapidly go out of alignment. Please don't turn it on for more than a second to check the current."

"Right. I'll take care of it personally. And I'd like

to add, Miss Gompers, that none of this would have been necessary if you people at the BBC had done your jobs properly."

"Be that as it may, Mr. St. Clair. I urge you to follow the instructions to the letter. Otherwise, you'll blow it."

Edgar St. Clair was a career man. His very first job was in the stock room at Harrods and now he was Manager of Special Events. He lived in the same flat in which he had grown up, from which he had buried his parents, and to which he had brought his wife, and their children. At forty-nine, with thinning blond hair, a huge handlebar mustache, and the inside track on getting unclaimed custom clothes from Harrods, Edgar St. Clair was not about to take any chances with the only special event he had scheduled for the month. He personally carried the mixer out of his office preceded by his secretary, who opened the door for him, pressed the button for the elevator, and stood guard as they went down to the auditorium.

They entered from the side and walked up the steps to the stage. She walked briskly and took the electric mixer that was already on the counter and moved it away so that he could put the new one down promptly. St. Clair sighed as he let go of it, careful not to shake it and distress the beaters. The auditorium, which sat about four hundred, was dotted with cleaning ladies, cameramen, and florists.

"Put the other machine backstage," he said. "I don't want any slip-ups." His secretary nodded and disappeared with the old mixer. St. Clair plugged in the replacement and turned it on to ensure that the outlet was working. He then turned it off. "Attention please, ladies and gentlemen. I have an announcement to make." He waited for all eyes to be turned toward him. "No one is to touch any of the equipment onstage. I have myself positioned and checked everything. The success of our demonstration today depends upon your cooperation in each keeping to his own task. Thank you."

There was a slight murmur and then the cleaning ladies went back to dusting the chairs, and the cameramen began shouting as they set up their lights. St. Clair took a deep breath. Opening-night jitters. Clearly that afternoon's special event would be a milestone. Never before had the BBC covered one of these events, and word was spreading that St. Clair was due for a position on the board. "The programs," he shouted as his secretary walked back onstage, "where are the programs?"

"They're here, Mr. St. Clair," said a clerk in the auditorium. "I've just begun putting one on each seat."

"Good," St. Clair said. "Nothing must go wrong today."

St. Clair and his secretary left the auditorium and went back to their office. The young man worked his way across the front row. On each seat he carefully put a program. The cover said:

Harrods,

in co-operation with LUCULLUS magazine,

are proud to present

Miss Natasha O'Brien,

famed international food expert,

in a demonstration of the dessert
prepared for Her Majesty Queen Elizabeth II
LA BOMBE RICHELIEU

The cover had on it a large picture of Natasha.
Smiling.

Bill Darling,

Oh, for the life of a literary agent! Just sitting there while all your slaves work and send you ten percent. Well, sweetness, if you've been expecting ten percent of my fee for the Good Morning Show, cancel your order for monogrammed jockey shorts.

I don't know how much news has hit New York, but my stepfather and two dear friends have been murdered rather brutally in what appears to be a vendetta against the great chefs of Europe. Even more extraordinary is the fact that yours truly appears to be a) the prime suspect and/or b) the next victim. (My God I'm not even a citizen of the country of Europe!)

Here's what I want you to do for me:

1. Call the network. I can't do the script or the show. I don't even know when I'll be back.

2. Call the papers. I'm on extended holiday or something. Anticipating your grubby mentality, I do not want to do restaurant reviews while I'm sitting around waiting to be shot. Nor do I want to write about the current state of gastronomy in Poland, or the problems of this year's rosé vintage. I want to do nothing for a while. Presuming I have a "while" in which to do nothing. (Won't you cry like a baby if this is my last letter before I'm brutally bumped off? Well, comfort yourself, I've left you my avocado plants and roaches.)

3. Call the publishers. If I live, I want to do a book called "Three Cooks" in which the recipes and lives of the three murdered chefs will be chronicled. There's a good deal of interweaving to be done, and I think we can hit both the cookbook and nonfiction markets. There now, doesn't that make you feel better? I bet you've got an erection already. Speaking of which,

4. Call your doctor. Find out about having yourself circumcised. Would you believe there are circumcised Italians? (Or am I just naïve?)

Well, there you are. (All shrunk up by now, eh?) I want to do the book very much. I have no doubt they will pick it up. After all, what has Simca got that I don't?

I know. Julia.

Write to me. But check the obits daily. No sense
wasting postage.

The late Natasha O'Brien.

Dear Mrs. Benson:
Enclosed you will find a check for next month. I
don't really know when I will be back, since some
pressing matters have developed. I want to be sure
you're sending the mail to my attorney, and, most of
all, feeding Arnold. I miss him so. Strange how you
can get attached to a plant, but maybe that's a sign
of maturity. Anyway, please write and tell me if he
has any new shoots. Also, have you been taking your
arthritis pills? I shall be very angry with you, dear
Mrs. Benson, if you are not able to go square dancing
with me when I come back. Please drop me a line.

Natasha O'Brien

Dear Legal Eagle:
Is it adultery if you sleep with your own ex-
husband?
How do you annul a divorce? (Have you fainted?)
What the hell have you done about the papers on
Louis' estate? And the trust fund for Hildegarde?
How much money do I have in the bank? Are you
paying my bills? (Be sure you pay Bloomies; they get
cranky the quickest of all.) Have you opened any of
my love letters? Did I get any love letters?
How often must a U.S. citizen return to the U.S. in
order to keep citizenship? Have you missed me?
Wouldn't you just drop dead if I remarried Millie?
240

What would you do if I were the next one killed? And how would you help me if I'm arrested on suspicion of murder? Do you have any colleagues over here who could help me?

Why don't I hear from you?

N?

Dear Craig:

It seems there's just no way I can make your annual clambake. Please extend my thanks and apologies to Pierre and his family. Big kisses to you, and keep the South Shore on its toes.

Love,
Natasha

Dear New York Times Delivery Service:
Please stop.

Ms. N. O'Brien

atasha and Max were facing one another as they lay in bed. The telephone rang.

"Hello."

"Good morning, Mr. Ogden. Nine o'clock."

"Thanks." He hung up the receiver and put his arms back around Natasha. They had already been awake for an hour.

"You know," Max said quietly, "the nice thing about our getting married, and getting divorced, and then getting married again is that your initials stay the same. You don't have to change anything that's monogrammed."

"I didn't say I'd marry you."

"You will."

"My initials are still NO."

"Let's face it. You'll eventually marry. It might as well be someone with the right initials. Of course, you could marry Laurence Olivier or David Oistrakh or Peter O'Toole. But you can't marry anyone without an 'O.'"

"I don't want to get married."

"But you have to," Max said. "I'm pregnant."

She smiled and put her hand to his face. "How do you know?"

"Clearly," he said, hugging her tightly, "I am with child."

"That's a sexist remark."

"I know. Sometimes I can't help myself."

"I know. I love you anyway."

"There. You've said it."

"I do love you, Millie. But I don't want to marry you."

"Well," he said, getting up, "what the hell. You can still scrub my back. C'mon."

They walked into the bathroom. Natasha turned on the shower and let the warm water comfort her. Max stood next to her and massaged her neck for a moment. Then he took the bar of soap and lathered the washcloth. Once the cloth was soapy, he began rubbing her back, and then her arms. "Okay," he said. "Get ready for another sexist remark. It is time," he sang, "to shine up your medals. Turn around."

Natasha turned to him and Max gently put the cloth to her chest. While holding her shoulder with one hand, he rubbed the cloth first on one breast and then the other.

"Millie," she said, leaning her head on his hand, "you're a nice man."

"But?"

"No buts. I'm grateful to have you as a friend."

"Jesus. Overheard at Mayerling."

"I can't say what you want me to say."

"Then shut up," he said, handing her the washcloth and turning his back to her, "and scrub."

Natasha and Max, like two friendly cats of the same sex, washed one another. Each was confident about his own body. There were no secret blemishes, no unexplored areas, no limitations. Max washed every part of Natasha's body, and she did the same for him. They were caretakers, each tending a valuable property they coveted but did not own. It was a time in which to share self-pride, not mutual admiration.

Drying, however, was different. It was a time of isolated reflection. Natasha would feel her breasts, run her hands over her buttocks, rub her stomach, and press her palm against her vagina. Max would slap his chest, sometimes comb his pubic hair (once he had tried to part it in the center), pull gently at his penis, and while he dried himself he would cup one hand under his testicles and press them firmly.

They shared the mirror as he shaved and she combed her hair. "Are you very uptight?" he asked.

"Very."

"But you understand you're frightened by the concept, not because there's any imminent danger?"

"Yes."

"But knowing it doesn't help because you're giving me monosyllabic answers."

"Right." She leaned against his back, putting her arms around his waist. "Rationally, I know nothing will happen to me today. Rationally, I know I'll see you for dinner." She extended her hand down to his penis. "Rationally, I know we'll make love tonight. And tomorrow we'll go to the police." Feeling the start of his erection, she took her hand away and stepped back from him. "But rationally, I also know that someone wants to kill me."

"Then let's go to the police today. Now. To hell with Harrods. The ladies in funny hats can survive without your recipe."

"But I can't survive without them. I need to go, Millie. Fear has taken away my independence. You, of all people, know how I've fought for that independence. I've got to get back to who I am. I need to be in control of some part of my life again, even for only a few hours. Otherwise, I might as well be dead."

There was a knock at the door. Max wrapped a towel around his waist and opened it. The breakfast waiter stood next to his table while Lucino lifted the cloth and searched the utensils. "I will take it inside," Lucino said slowly. "You wait there." Then he looked at Max. "Where is she?"

"In the bathroom. She's fine. Everything is okay, Lucino. Thank you."

"Miss O'Brien?" he called.

"Good morning, darling," she replied. "Don't they ever let you sleep?"

"I told you," Max said. "She lives. Lucino, I'm on your side," Max confirmed. "Now thank you very much. And thank you, too," Max said to the nonplussed waiter standing in the hall. "Lucino," he said softly, "you'd better tip the waiter." Max closed the door.

"What's happening?" Natasha called.

"Nothing. It was just Lucino frisking the corn flakes."

Natasha sat on a pink velvet chair in the lobby, waiting for Achille. She wore her pink Chanel suit, and held tightly to her pink suede Hermès purse. At her feet was the red alligator knife case. She sat bolt upright, moving only her head as she watched people walk across the lobby. Max and Lucino were standing behind her, on either side of the chair.

"I feel as though we should have our picture taken," Max said.

"Do not take any pictures of me," Lucino warned.

"Right," Max said. "No pictures. No, sir."

"Millie, what time will you be back?"

Max bent over and kissed her. "I'm not going to Paris. I'll cancel. I'll stay with you."

She leaned toward him. "No, you mustn't. I'm safe today. Nothing can happen. Or don't you believe what you've been telling me?"

"Of course I believe it."

"Then go. If you stay, you'll only make me think there's something to worry about."

"That's not it. I just want to be with you. I know you're upset."

"Then give me confidence. Go to Paris."

Rudolph walked through the swinging door and

came over to them. "Good morning," he said brightly. "Mr. van Golk is in the car."

"Good morning," Natasha said, getting up. She took a deep breath and smiled at Max.

"So gimme a big fat one," he said, leaning over to kiss her.

"You already got a big fat one," she whispered. Then, without turning back, Natasha walked through the swinging door. Max waited in the lobby, watching as Rudolph opened the door and Natasha stepped into the black Rolls. Lucino sat up front with Rudolph. As they drove away, Max felt increasingly uneasy. Was he just lonely? He decided to call Paris and cancel his appointment. He would follow her to Harrods.

"Good morning, Citizen Publisher," Natasha said, settling in next to Achille. "Off to Madame La Guillotine?"

"I think not."

"Ah, but do you speak for yourself or for all of France?"

"I speak for the police."

"What do you mean?" she asked anxiously. "Have you thought of whom it might be?"

"Yes."

"Well, yes what?"

"Yes. I have thought about it."

"And?"

"And I in fact do know who the killer is."

She was afraid to ask. Suddenly she didn't want to know. Her eyes were riveted on Achille.

"The killer is Arnold Victor Tresting. A madman

who was treasurer for LUCULLUS. I dismissed him recently for gross insubordination. Seeking his revenge, in a manner befitting a treasurer, he determined to destroy those things I treasure the most. He is now in the custody of New Scotland Yard, having made a full confession."

Her mind repeated over and over again what Achille had just said. Arnold Victor Tresting. Treasurer. Confession. Arnold Victor Tresting. Destroy the Treasures. In Custody.

"Tresting never appeared to have any more imagination than an artichoke. I still cannot believe he was capable of such brilliant executions."

"He killed Louis, and Nutti, and Jean-Claude?"

"It appears he is a compulsive litterer."

"He confessed?"

"He confessed."

"And the police have him?"

"Must I hire a scribe?"

"Achille, is all this true?" She began laughing and crying. "They have the killer? I don't have to be afraid any longer?"

"My dear, I have personally seen to everything."

Natasha took a handkerchief from her purse. "Not that I was ever really frightened." She blew her nose and began crying loudly.

"I would never have credited Tresting with such creativity. However, after your having presented me with the theory that the killer was someone who wished revenge against me, I thought immediately of Tresting. I recalled that when I had dismissed him, he became enraged and shouted that he would have his revenge upon me. At the time, he was having an affair with one of my proofreaders. A match made in minutia heaven. She confirmed for him my preferences in chefs."

"Was he planning to kill me?"

"Yes."

"How?"

"It was his plan to lock you in a freezer."

"A freezer?" She put her hand to her mouth. "Where?"

"Presumably in London. Although his ingenuity is difficult to anticipate."

"Ingenuity? He's crazy."

"The man is a genius!"

"Achille," she said angrily. "Three men have been killed."

"Indeed. But you must admit he performed with great *éclat*."

"I can't believe you. I can't believe what I'm hearing. You're obviously very upset, Achille."

"Of course, I'm upset. This is rather an embarrassment for me. A member of my own staff."

"Why didn't you call me? Oh, poor Millie, he doesn't know. Why did you wait to tell me?"

"I have just come from Scotland Yard. In truth, I was instructed to say nothing. There is still the possibility, albeit remote, that Tresting did not act alone. Therefore, we must not relax our security, or risk the possibility of a leak."

"The proofreader?"

"She has not been located as yet."

"Then I'm not safe?"

"You are perfectly safe. We are simply taking precautions. No mere proofreader could have devised such a plan. For the time being, no one must know about Tresting. Especially Lucino. His mentality can deal only in absolutes."

"Mine, too."

"He is in custody. Tresting cannot harm you."

"Tresting has already harmed me."

"I do not want anything said until we are out of Harrods. Do you understand?"

"Yes. But the moment I'm through, I'm calling Millie."

"The moment you're safely out of Harrods, you may do anything you wish."

"Does he have a family?"

"Tresting? Yes."

"How terrible for them."

"I suppose you wish me to initiate a trust fund for Kids of Killers."

She smiled and sat back thinking how lucky she was to have a friend like Achille. Perhaps he could help her reconstruct her life. Perhaps she'd take a job at LUCULLUS, live in London, near Hildegarde, and begin repairing the damage she'd caused. And she'd be close enough to Max not to have to marry him. She thought of Louis. Would she ever stop thinking of Louis? Someone had stolen him from her past and made him an intruder on her future. "Achille, I keep thinking that the name Arnold Victor Tresting means nothing to me. What does he look like?"

"He has one eye, a hook for a hand, and a wooden leg."

"This security business. I mean, there is no danger, is there? Tresting *is* the one. It's just to clear up loose ends. Now that they have Tresting, there's no one else, is there?"

"My dear Natasha, were there two Leonardos?"

The car pulled up in front of Harrods. Lucino ran out even before Rudolph had stopped completely, and brushed aside the doorman. Natasha took Lucino's hand and got out of the car. Rudolph leaned in to extract Achille.

"Be back in an hour and wait for me," he told Rudolph.

Natasha kissed Achille on the cheek. "Did I ever tell you that I love you?" She put her arm in his and together they walked into the store. Natasha stopped in front of a large sign announcing that Natasha O'Brien, international food expert, would be appearing in the auditorium. "She's so pretty," Natasha said, looking at her own picture, "and such a nice person too."

They walked to the elevator and were pressed in among a gaggle of weekday shoppers. From the back of the crowd Natasha heard a whispered "That's 'er. There she is." When they reached the fourth floor, they were met by Edgar St. Clair, who had given instructions to the doorman to notify him upon Natasha's arrival.

"Miss O'Brien, welcome to Harrods. What an honor for us to have you here today. And Mr. van Golk, how good to see you again."

"Indeed. I shall browse amongst the petticoats until show time." He kissed Natasha on the cheek. "Don't disgrace Daddy."

"You're really staying for it?" she asked.

"I wouldn't miss it for the world." Achille turned and walked down the corridor.

Lucino tugged at Natasha's arm. "What is it?"

"I want to frisk him."

"No. No frisking, Lucino. Just go and sit out front. You'll be able to see everything."

"I'll go with you."

"Only until I'm onstage. Then down, Lucino. And now, Mr. St. Clair, may I see the kitchen, please?"

"Of course. I think you'll find a surprise in store for you." He ushered her through a narrow corridor leading to a flight of stairs. "I must say I'm amazed we managed to get anything done with the BBC people mucking up all about us. You have no idea how inefficient they are." He decided not to tell her about the incident with the mixer.

The auditorium was ablaze with lights. Bearded young men in torn sweaters were yelling "Get rid of that bloody shadow," "How the fuck many eggs does she need?," "If you don't get that camera out of the way, you'll be taking a picture of my ass." Somewhere amid the cameras and the four monitors and the endless stream of cables and invectives and commands, somewhere amid the litter of empty paper coffee cups and cigarette butts, fogged in by a layer of stale cigarette smoke, was the kitchen set. As per Natasha's written instructions, there was a work area on stage left (stove, refrigerator-freezer, sink, electric mixer, pots, whisks, etc.) and an assembly area on stage right (counter, refrigerator-freezer, molds, trays, knives, etc.). A single microphone was suspended above each work area, and a desk microphone was placed atop a lectern at center stage. A very flustered Miss Beauchamp was standing in the work area, holding a mixing bowl to her chest while someone behind a camera yelled, "All I'm getting is tits."

Natasha walked briskly to center stage and tapped the microphone. "Testing, testing, one, two, three," she said tentatively. She smiled broadly as she began to speak. "Good afternoon. My name is Natasha O'Brien. The next cocksucker who says 'tits' will get thrown out of here on his ass. You may feel free to use the full range of expletives from 'damn' to 'fuck.' As for the mammary and vaginal areas of the female form, cool it. It pisses me off and I'm sure it disturbs the very nice lady who has been patiently standing under these lights. I'll look forward to meeting each of you personally in a few minutes. Thank you."

There was complete silence as Natasha walked across the stage. Edgar St. Clair stood against a refrigerator, both palms pressed against the door.

"Miss Beauchamp," Natasha said, embracing her. "I'm so pleased you're here."

"And I'm so relieved to see you. I've been your stand-in for nearly an hour and I'm ready for medical aid."

"I'm sorry. Mr. St. Clair, why isn't this place air-conditioned? Will you please turn it on at once? Full up. And please get your cleaning people in here on the double." St. Clair, his ears still ringing from Natasha's inaugural address, nodded and gladly disappeared.

"You look smashing," Miss Beauchamp said.

"You should be ashamed of yourself for looking so well."

"You are a love. Tell me, where is the *Bombe*?"

"It's the best *Bombe* I've ever seen! Mr. Cornwell," she called into the wings, "may we have a word with you?" Jacques Cornwell was a short, fat man whose bald head was covered with perspiration. He was dressed in a white chef's coat and trousers. "Miss O'Brien, Mr. Cornwell. Without his help behind the scenes, this afternoon would not have been possible."

"Mr. Cornwell," Natasha said, shaking his hand. "A pleasure, and thank you."

"I have admired you for years, Miss O'Brien. No one understands egg yolks the way you do. I do hope I've done you justice."

"I think it's I who must do you justice, Mr. Cornwell. Well. Shall we see how the Cardinal is doing?" He took a deep apprehensive breath and opened the door to the freezer. Natasha watched as the cold air fogged and wafted out. She envisioned him taking her body out of the cold deadly darkness of the freezer. Involuntarily, her hand went to her forehead.

"Something wrong?" Miss Beauchamp asked. "Need some headache tablets?"

"No. Thank you. If only it were a headache."

Cornwell brought out *La Bombe Richelieu*. A spun sugar crown sat atop an ornate mold of raspberry ice surrounded by a ring of whipped cream into which fresh raspberries were positioned like jewels. "Oh, it's beautiful," she said. "Mr. Cornwell, it's perfect."

"I simply followed your instructions," he said,

beaming. He turned the plate around to show he had cut a wedge from the mold. Beneath the raspberry ice was a layer of chocolate almond ice cream, and at the center of the *Bombe,* a frozen yellow mousse studded with bits of chocolate.

"Fit for a Queen," Natasha said. "I can't wait to taste it." Cornwell took a plate from the freezer containing the wedge he had cut. Natasha picked at the whipped cream and tasted it. "God, you have great cows over here. If only we had cream like this in the States." Cornwell was smiling. She tasted the mousse mixture, hesitated, and then tasted it again. "That's not right."

Cornwell lowered his eyes. "I thought it was delicious."

"You used Curaçao instead of Gran Marnier." He shrugged his shoulders. She tasted the chocolate ice cream and licked her lips rapidly. "And you used packaged chocolate," she said unbelievingly. "I specifically said freshly made unwrapped chocolate."

"I thought it was delicious," Cornwell said.

"Mr. Cornwell, please don't lead me to the obvious comment about the physical location of your taste buds."

"I am sorry," he said.

"I'm sorry," Miss Beauchamp said. "I told everyone to follow your instructions to the letter."

"I know you did, darling. It's not your fault. There's no real harm done. Thank God no one has to eat any of it." She threw the plate into the garbage.

"So you see," Cornwell said, "it does not matter that I use this or that. It matters only that it looks well."

"Well, a Nietzsche in chef's clothing? Sorry, Mr. Cornwell, I don't buy your politics any more than I buy your chocolate." She walked past him, taking Miss Beauchamp by the hand. "We'd better check everything out right now."

Natasha nodded and smiled at the cameraman as she and Miss Beauchamp stepped over the cables and made their way to the work area. She turned the faucets on and off. She lit the stove and turned it off. She put her hand on the bowl of eggs to feel their temperature. She poked a fork into the sugar to make certain there were no lumps, and then opened the refrigerator to smell the cream and examine the raspberries. She flipped the mixer on and off.

Natasha turned quickly and found herself facing a short, middle-aged man with a head of very curly brown hair that fell to his shoulders. "I am Morris Mayfield. What have they been telling you about me?"

"*The* Morris Mayfield?" she said in surprise. She extended her hand to shake his. "I'm one of your biggest fans. I've always respected the brutal honesty of your films. But surely you're not . . ."

"A director is a director, Miss . . . Miss . . ."

"O'Brien."

"Whatever." A tall, slender young man whispered something into Mayfield's ear while he put his hand on his shoulder. Mayfield nodded and the young man sauntered away. "As though you didn't know, I am in the midst of my fourth divorce, in the midst of drying out from a rather alcoholic summer, and in the midst of my first homosexual affair. My analyst suggested I take this offer from the BBC to re-establish

256

my credibility. Do you think I was right in taking his advice?"

"Well, I don't know. . . ."

"I might as well tell you that Sergio does all the cooking. I have taken the traditional male role in our relationship. Do you think I should have taken the female role?"

"Mr. Mayfield, I don't know. . . ."

"You appear to be a very strong woman. My analyst claims that my four marriages failed because I refused to accept the fact that I need a stronger woman. He thinks it's very healthy for me to have this relationship with Sergio. What do you think?"

"I think, Mr. Mayfield, that we had better proceed with the day's occupation."

"Are you rejecting me?"

"Mr. Mayfield . . ."

"Yes, you are. You're rejecting me because you feel threatened by my homosexual alliance."

"I do not feel threatened, Mr. Mayfield, by anything other than the immediate pressure of time. I would like to walk through this with you so that . . ."

"You wouldn't tell me the truth anyway. Women never do."

Natasha put her hand to her forehead and leaned on the counter. She took a deep breath of exasperation and shrugged her shoulders. Looking him directly in the eyes, she began to speak in a low, tense voice. "Mr. Mayfield, you are right. I reject you. You are a threat to me, a threat to my raspberries, and a threat to the self-esteem of my vulva. To tell the truth, Mr. Mayfield, you absolutely terrify me."

"But do I disgust you?"

"You bet."

A thin smile stretched his lips, and his eyes began to glisten. "I've spent over a week reading your recipe. It's quite sensual. The mingling of colors and textures is perfect. Well," he said, smiling brightly, "enough of this chitchat. I'd suggest we have a run-through."

Natasha smiled. "I'm ready for my close-up, Mr. Mayfield."

"All right, you buggers," he yelled. "Let's clear the bloody set." Mayfield walked away from Natasha and began moving the crew about.

"How's the temperature now?" St. Clair asked, reappearing behind her.

"Terrific."

"Miss O'Brien," Lucino called. "I want the lights in the auditorium to stay on."

"Oh, Lucino!"

"Miss O'Brien, will you say a few words so we can adjust the volume on the mike?"

"Miss O'Brien, will you be wearing an apron?"

"Miss O'Brien, do you ever go back to stage left once the assembly has begun?"

"Miss O'Brien, how close to the mixer will you be standing?"

Natasha walked under the microphone. "My name is Natasha O'Brien."

"Louder, please."

"My name is Natasha O'Brien," she said as her voice filled the auditorium, "and I want to go home."

"That's fine. We got it."

"Miss O'Brien," Mayfield called to her, "we're ready when you are."

Natasha walked to stage left. "We begin with my being introduced by Mr. St. Clair. There will be a round of tumultuous applause. I enter from stage left and walk to center stage front. Then"—she began pacing out the steps she would take—"I go to the fridge in the assembly area and show the final product. A few words, blah, blah, blah, and then back to the work area. I separate the eggs and put the yolks into the mixer bowl. Then I beat the eggs in the mixer for about three minutes."

"Can you make it two minutes?" Mayfield asked. "There's nothing terribly visual about your standing in front of the mixer."

"Three minutes, Mr. Mayfield."

"I suppose we could pan to the audience. You know, Miss O'Brien, three minutes is a crashing bore."

"Well, you can always cut to pages falling off a calendar."

"We'll work it out."

St. Clair tiptoed over to her. "It's very late, Miss O'Brien. We have quite a crowd gathering outside."

"Lucino," she called, "he's bothering me." St. Clair stepped back as Lucino approached.

"When do you make the pretty red ices?" Mayfield asked.

"I'm not making any ices. That's already been done. I'm simply making the *mousse* mixture and the spun sugar cap. The rest is an assembly job. It takes place here on stage right."

"Well, then, what about the chocolate? I have

259

three pages of camera angles on the melting of the chocolate."

"Save them for Masterpiece Theatre."

"Mr. St. Clair," someone called from the back of the auditorium. "Mr. St. Clair, when can I let them in?"

"Let's not be snotty, Miss O'Brien," Mayfield said sharply. "Please try to harness your aggressions so they do not interfere with our work."

"I'm trying, Mr. Mayfield. God knows I'm trying."

"Good. Just have faith in us."

"Mr. Mayfield," she said wearily, "this is Harrods, not Lourdes."

"We're late," St. Clair said.

"Miss O'Brien, when the little red light goes on . . ."

"I smile."

"As you wish. May I suggest we get on with it then? You'll only be in two areas and we'll follow you. Whatever we don't get the first time, we can take later. Sort of a semi-*cinéma vérité.*"

"Half-baked," Natasha murmured.

"Don't worry. You do your thing and I'll do mine. I know what I'm doing. By God, it's good to be back!"

Natasha saw Achille take a seat in the back row, on the aisle.

"Miss O'Brien, I must insist we begin," St. Clair said timidly.

"Then rap three times, and bring on the broads." Natasha walked offstage.

The doors were opened and within moments the auditorium was filled with chattering women. St. Clair ran backstage to Natasha. "Why must the auditorium lights remain on? I can't talk to your man. He's threatened to knock me unconscious."

"Then you'd better leave the lights on."

"Who is he?"

"He is trying to protect me from a mad killer."

"Really," St. Clair humphed.

Miss Beauchamp took Natasha's arm. "I know everything will go swimmingly."

"Of course it will," St. Clair snipped. "We've worked very hard to ensure the success of this afternoon. And we've worked against odds on which we had not counted. Firstly, there was the problem with your mixer . . ."

"What problem?"

"Don't fret. It's all taken care of."

"Mr. St. Clair, I don't know what you're talking about." Natasha began brushing her hair.

"And then the business with Mr. Cornwell."

"He didn't follow the goddamn recipe. All he had to do was read."

"And then the air conditioning. And then the camera crew. And then your friend . . ."

"Mr. St. Clair, let's have a truce. You just move your ass out there and introduce me, and I'll take care of the rest."

"Really!" he said. "Miss Gompers was certainly right about you."

"Who the hell is Miss Gompers?" she asked. St. Clair curled his lip, pulled his jacket straight, smiled, and walked onstage. There was a smattering of applause. "Welcome, shoppers," she heard him begin.

"Are you all right?" Miss Beauchamp whispered to Natasha.

"I don't know. My nerves are so raw."

"Small wonder."

"But at least we know everything is under control."

St. Clair had begun his introduction. "And we are indeed fortunate that Miss O'Brien has consented to share with us her original recipe for the *Bombe* that . . ."

"Miss Beauchamp, tell me," Natasha asked hesitantly, "did you know Tresting?"

"Tresting?" She looked incredulous. "Yes, of course. But how would you know . . ."

"Never mind how I know. What kind of man is he?"

"The most charitable word is boring."

"Boring?"

"And so, ladies," St. Clair continued, "it is with the greatest of pleasure . . ."

"Well, with the condition his heart was in, I'd be surprised if he could stand the excitement of a crossword puzzle."

"Arnold Victor Tresting?" Natasha said to verify they were speaking of the same person.

"Miss Natasha O'Brien!" There was a prolonged applause, during which Natasha stood staring at Miss Beauchamp, who finally gave her a nudge. Natasha walked onstage smiling.

"Thank you. Thank you very much." Her mind was in a frenzy. Something was wrong. "I had the pleasure recently of having been invited . . ."

Outside the auditorium, Max was stopped by a guard. "I'm sorry, sir, but the hall is full up."

"I'm her husband."

"Oh, I see. Well, I'm afraid there are no seats, Mr. O'Brien."

Max winced. "I'll just stand in the back."

"Right, sir."

Max opened the door and was surprised to find the house lights on. He watched Natasha as she described the kitchen at Buckingham Palace.

She saw Max walk in and stand in the back. She continued talking, not listening to herself, aware only that something must be terribly wrong if Max was there. The audience laughed as she described her problem in getting the ice cream away from the waiters before they ate it all. She paused. The word "boring" kept reverberating in her mind. Why the hell was Max there?

"However," she said brightly, "food triumphs over evil." She opened the freezer. *"La Bombe Richelieu."* There were oohs and aahs, as she held the dessert aloft to allow Mayfield's crew to photograph it. Then she turned it around to where the wedge had been removed. "But even Cardinal Richelieu has something under his hat. And that's where our demonstration will begin. With the basic *mousse* mixture."

Outside the auditorium, Hildegarde was stopped. "I'm sorry, madam, but the hall is full up."

"But she's my *Tochter.*"

"Pardon?"

"I'm her mother."

First the husband, now the mother. "Oh, I see. Well, I'm afraid there are no seats."

"I have feet. I'll stand." Hildegarde opened the door and found herself standing next to Max. They smiled at one another. He leaned over to kiss her on the cheek.

"Having washed my hands," Natasha said, drying them with a towel, "we'll begin by separating the eggs." She cracked an egg on the edge of the bowl. Mayfield moved in for a close-up. Natasha opened the egg into her palm, careful to cup the yolk. The white ran out between her fingers. After she received the appropriate murmur from the audience, she said, "I find this far and away the best way to separate eggs." Mayfield, not having expected anything as earthy, was poking his crew to keep focused on her hands. "Frankly, I'm just not the type to keep shifting the yolk from shell to shell." Natasha looked up and saw Hildegarde standing next to Max. "Excuse me," she said, walking to the front of the stage. "Mami?"

All heads turned toward the back of the auditorium. Hildegarde smiled shyly and waved. "Someone very special to me has just come in. I would very much like you to meet the person who taught me how to cook. I would like you to meet my mother, Hildegarde Kohner." There was a burst of applause. Mayfield was annoyed that he had to divert one camera to follow Natasha as she started down the steps that led from the stage. She stretched her hand toward Hildegarde, urging her to come forward.

Achille felt himself breathing rapidly.

"Mami," Natasha called. "Please." And then, to the audience, "How'd you like to see a mother-and-daughter act?" There was wild applause, and

Mayfield began jumping up and down with excitement at the *vérité* of it all. Max started to push Hildegarde down the aisle. "C'mon, Mami, let's show them. Together."

Natasha walked toward Hildegarde and embraced her. The two women stood in the middle of the auditorium hugging one another and crying. The applause was truly tumultuous, and Mayfield's crew ran about as though they were covering a rock festival. Natasha and Hildegarde walked up the steps, their arms around one another. "I never dreamed you'd come," Natasha whispered.

"Tochter, I got your letter. With that letter there is no place I wouldn't go. We will be together from now on. *Ja?"*

"Oh, Mami." Natasha hugged her. "We'll have such a wonderful life together." With tears streaming down her face, Natasha stepped forward. "I must apologize, but I'm as surprised as you. However, if you'll just give us a minute, I promise you a *Bombe* you won't ever forget." Again, there was excited applause.

Natasha gave Hildegarde a copy of the recipe. Hildegarde read it, nodding her head as she took off her coat and pushed up her sleeves. Mayfield motioned for Natasha to move into the assembly area, while Hildegarde settled into the work area at stage left. Two cameramen were center stage, back to back— one covering Hildegarde, and the other, Natasha. Hildegarde washed her hands quickly and nodded that she was ready.

Achille stood up and put his hand to his chest. He grew fearful at the beating of his heart and only half heard what was being said because of the pounding in his ears. He began walking backward, his hands searching the wall until he felt a doorknob.

"Once the eggs are separated," Natasha said, standing behind the counter at stage right, "we slip the yolks into the bowl."

Achille watched, unblinking, as Hildegarde put the egg yolks into the electric mixer.

"And now, the eggs must be beaten until they are thick." Hildegarde turned on the mixer. Mayfield signaled to cut the sound from her microphones. "You'll find this takes anywhere from two to three minutes before you get them a nice pale yellow. After the eggs are beaten fully, we'll add the sugar syrup that's been made by boiling two-thirds of a cup of granulated sugar in one-third of a cup of water. How are the eggs coming?"

"Soon," Hildegarde said. "They are still too much the color of a sunset. They must be a sunrise."

The explosion blew off Hildegarde's head and arms. Pieces of the mixer and the camera hurtled into the audience. The cameraman was thrown to the floor with fragments of steel embedded in his face. Mayfield screamed, holding his hands in front of his eyes, the blood gushing down his arms. Natasha was thrown behind the counter, protected from flying debris by the double rank of cameras between stage left and stage right. Max yelled, "Nat, Nat," fighting his way down the aisle as screaming women, some bleeding profusely, pushed their way out of the auditorium.

Achille stepped backward through the exit. In the panic he was unnoticed as he proceeded to the elevator and down to the main floor. He walked out a side door and hailed a taxi.

"Fifteen Hertford Street," he said. "I want to pick something up. I'll give you twenty pounds if you hurry. Then wait for me."

"Twenty pounds? Yes, sir!"

"Hurry! Hurry!" Achille could hardly breathe. He was sweating so profusely that his vision became blurred. There was no way to have anticipated Hildegarde, he kept telling himself. But what could he tell Estella?

LA BOMBE RICHELIEU

1. *Frozen Mousse Mixture*

    2/3 cup sugar
    1/3 cup water

    Make sugar syrup.

    8 egg yolks

    Beat egg yolks in electric mixer until pale yellow. Continue beating while slowly pouring in thin stream of sugar syrup. Beat until mixture is thick.

    1 1/2 cups
    heavy cream
    2 T minced
    orange peel
    2 T Gran Marnier
    (or to taste)
    3 T chopped fresh
    unwrapped
    semisweet choco-
    late

    Whip cream until stiff. Add other ingedients. Fold into egg mixture.

    1 egg white

    Beat egg white until stiff. Fold into mixture. Freeze.

2. *Raspberry Ice*

    2 cups sugar
    4 cups water

    Make sugar syrup.

2 quarts fresh raspberries	Pound berries through a sieve.
1/3 cup Framboise	Add Framboise and juice
2 lemons	from lemons.
	Add equal amount of sugar syrup to fruit mix. Freeze.

3. *Chocolate Almond Ice Cream*

4 cups milk vanilla bean	Boil milk with vanilla bean. Remove bean.
1 2/3 cups grated fresh unwrapped semisweet chocolate	Dissolve chocolate into 1 cup boiling water, then mix into milk.
1 cup sugar	Beat sugar into egg yolks
10 egg yolks	until thick. Add chocolate mixture to egg yolks. Cook until mix coats the spoon. Do not boil. Pour through a sieve into a bowl.
2/3 cup fresh almonds	Blanch and crush almonds. Add to mixture. Let cool. Stir occasionally. Freeze in usual manner.

4. *Whipped Cream*

| 2 cups heavy cream | Whip cream and sugar over ice until stiff. Refrigerate. |
| 1/4 cup confectioners' sugar | |

5. *Spun Sugar Crown*

1 cup sugar	Mix corn syrup and water.
1/3 cup hot water	Add liquid to sugar. Boil
1/4 cup corn syrup	until mix turns caramel
	color. Cool until slightly
	thick. Dip fork in syrup
	and wave over inverted
	oiled metal bowl that is
	larger than bombe mold.
	Repeat dipping and waving
	until threads collect and a
	cage is formed. When
	sugar is cool, remove crown
	from bowl. Refrigerate.

ASSEMBLY

1. Line bombe mold with layer of raspberry ice. Freeze.
2. Line with layer of chocolate ice cream. Freeze.
3. Fill center with frozen mousse mixture. Freeze.
4. Spread chocolate ice cream across bottom. Freeze.
5. Immediately before serving fill pastry tube (medium scallop) with whipped cream.
6. Unmold *Bombe.* Make decorative ring of whipped cream around base of *Bombe.* Top *Bombe* with peak of whipped cream.
7. Dot cream with perfect fresh raspberries.
8. Put spun sugar crown atop *Bombe.* Serve at once. Cut with serrated knife.

Wine: d'Yquem. If economizing, serve champagne.

chille got out of the taxi the moment it stopped at 15 Hertford Street. In the elevator he readied his keys to open the door, and stepping over Cesar, he hurried to the desk and grabbed his passport. Cesar meowed. Achille hesitated, went into the kitchen, took the entire bowl of chopped shrimp, and left it on the floor. He walked out of the flat without stopping to lock up.

Once in the taxi, he told the driver to take him to Heathrow, international departures terminal.

"Yes, sir. For twenty pounds, I'll take you to the moon."

Achille sank back, the blood pounding in his temples. He thought only of Estella. What could he tell her?

"Mr. van Golk? It's not Thursday!" the ticket clerk said.

"I know."

"I hope nothing's wrong with Mrs. van Golk."

"It's an emergency."

"Let me see if Flight 68 has taken off yet. Perhaps I can hold it." She picked up the telephone. "Hello, I have an emergency VIP. Can you hold sixty-eight? Just long enough to get through passport control. He's right here. Thank you."

She stepped around the counter and took Achille by the arm, noticing how pale and shaken he was. "Let me help you, Mr. van Golk. You look rather upset."

"Thank you."

"Mrs. van Golk must be a wonderful woman. Your devotion is legendary."

They arrived at passport control. "Why, Mr. van Golk, it's not Thursday," the inspector said. "I hope there's not something wrong."

"We're holding Flight 68. Can we hurry, please?" she asked.

"Of course. May I just have your passport and ticket, Mr. van Golk?"

Achille reached into his pocket and gave the inspector his passport. "I have no ticket," he said.

"There's no time. We'll put it on your account."

The inspector stamped his passport. "I hope . . . I mean . . . I'm sorry."

The girl held Achille's arm and led him through

the empty check-in lounge and down the stairs to the waiting VIP car. She helped him inside and gave the driver instructions. When they reached the plane, the three stewardesses from first class waited atop the ramp to glimpse the VIP.

"Mr. van Golk!" Miss Schnee called out. "Oh, my God. It's finally happened." She ran down the steps to help Achille up the ramp. "Clear out row A," she called to the other stewardesses. "You poor man, you look dreadful. I know I shouldn't ask, but is it . . . is it over?"

Achille looked at her and shook his head yes.

"Oh, I am so very sorry. Is there something I can do?" she asked.

"Leave me alone," he said. "Alone."

"But Mr. van Golk, it's not Thursday!" The Swiss immigration officer looked first at Achille and then at Miss Schnee, who motioned him to keep quiet. "I'm sorry," he said. Achille walked through immigration to customs.

"But Mr. van Golk, it's not Thursday!" Miss Schnee motioned to hush the customs inspector. She and Achille passed through and walked to the taxi stand. "Shall I go with you?" Miss Schnee asked. Achille looked at her with contempt and ripped her hand from his arm. She stood speechless, frozen by the anger in his eyes. He stepped into a taxi.

"Bonjour, monsieur."

"The Enstein Clinic. Hurry."

"But Achille, it's not Thursday!" Estella van Golk stood in the doorway to her room. "You've made a terrible mistake."

Estella was an incredibly beautiful woman, taller

than Achille and with the bearing of an Austrian empress. Her flaming red hair was parted in the center and fell about her shoulders in masses. Her oval face belied her more than fifty years. She wore no makeup to cover her luminous pink skin and naturally rouged cheeks. Her eyes were enormous, bright, blue, and clear. She wore an ankle-length, pale-blue satin smock that tied at the neck in a large floppy bow. She turned her back and walked into the room. She moved with a slender grace punctuated by the sweeping gestures of her outstretched arms.

Estella's room did not belong in the rarefied atmosphere of a sterile Swiss clinic for the insane. Originally two rooms, she and Achille had spent months redesigning the space into a combination bedroom, parlor, and office. The ceiling and walls were pale blue and matched the broadloom. A bright-blue floral-print fabric was set into the panels on the walls. It was used again as drapes, and also gathered itself atop Estella's bed as a canopy. Blue vases overflowed with yellow roses. A double glass door opened onto a terrace that offered an uncluttered vista of blue sky and white-capped Alps. In one corner of the room was Estella's French provincial desk and a series of file cabinets that had been covered in drapery fabric. The desk was cluttered with galley sheets, color separations, and photographer's proofs.

"Just how much more of your bumbling must I take?"

"What have you heard?" he asked, nearly collapsing onto the sofa.

"There's nothing I need to hear." Estella walked behind her desk and lit a cigarette. "I still have eyes. I can see." She pointed to the galleys and photo

274

proofs. "I can see, Achille, that the Easter issue is a disaster. I simply will not approve it for printing." She put her palms on the desk, leaned forward menacingly and shouted, "There are seven typographical errors!"

"I'm sorry, Estella."

"Sorry? Don't you think it's a bit late to be sorry? There are seven mistakes, Achille. Do you know how many mistakes that makes so far this year?" She turned to her file cabinet and took a ring of keys from her pocket. She unlocked the top drawer. It was empty except for a single sheet of paper. "One hundred and twelve," she said, waving the paper. "Of which the most misspellings are words beginning with B, L, and D. Why those letters, Achille?"

"I don't know."

"Don't know or won't tell? Which is it?"

"I have no secrets from you, Estella."

"You know what this means."

"Another list."

"Yes. But, I wasn't expecting you today. I'll write it now. So that you don't forget, my little bumbler bee." Estella slammed shut her file drawer and locked it. She sat down at her desk and took a piece of pale-blue notepaper. She dipped her pale-blue quill pen into a crystal inkwell filled with blue ink. She wrote in a large hand, scratching angrily at the paper. Estella rose and walked to Achille. She handed it to him. He looked at the message. Scrawled across the page was KILL THE PROOFREADER KILL THE TYPOGRAPHER. "I can't be certain which of them is more responsible for the errors so you'd best kill them both."

He stared into Estella's eyes, eyes that had once looked at him so adoringly. He searched for compassion, but found only rage. Estella stopped at the window on her way back to her desk. She leaned against the terrace door and stared out at the mountains. "It doesn't even look like Thursday. Why are you here today? Why are you here on the wrong day?"

"I wanted to be with you."

After a long moment, she turned from the window. Her face was beaming. "Poor bear, it must be so lonely for you. But I'll be home soon." She walked to the sofa and sat next to him. "It will be as we remembered it. Lying on our bed. Sipping champagne. Proofreading together till dawn."

Achille raised his arm and put it around Estella. Despite the pain, his fingers pressed greedily at the satin to feel the outline of Estella's shoulder. "Estella, I miss you so much."

"Tell me, darling, how has your week been? Did you kill Natasha?"

He pulled his arm away and walked to the window. "No."

"Did you say *no?*" she asked unbelievingly.

"I did not kill Natasha."

"But why not? You got my instructions?"

"Yes."

"There were no errors in them. I proofread them a dozen times to make certain. Why didn't you use the mixer?"

"I didn't say I didn't use it."

"Well, then she is dead. Dinner is over." Estella got up and went to Achille. "I am so very proud of you, darling. Killing the chefs may have been your idea for a foolproof diet, but I devised the plans so brilliantly. We should really write it up for one of the medical journals."

"Natasha isn't dead. The mixer killed the wrong person."

"What? You made a mistake, Achille?"

"I did not make a mistake. There was simply nothing I could do. Everything had been set up perfectly. Then, at the last minute, someone else turned the mixer on. I did not make the mistake, Estella. Something unforeseen happened at the last moment."

"That, Achille, for your future reference, is known as a mistake. Something that happens at the last moment contrary to one's plan is a mistake and you have made a mistake. Oh my God. After all I went through! To have you make a mistake at the last minute. Oh, how like you that is, Achille. You send me corrected galleys and I find seven mistakes in them. I suppose I shouldn't have expected you to carry out the killing of the chefs any better than you carry out the preparation of your manuscripts."

"Estella, listen to me. There was nothing I could do."

"Life is filled with alternatives, Achille. I'm sure you could have done something. Surely you could have done something other than come here to upset me. And you came here on the wrong day!"

"Estella, the mixer, and not I, killed the wrong person."

"An innocent person?"

"Yes."

"Dreadful." Estella walked to her desk and sat down. "The most dreadful mistake of all." She put her hand to her forehead. "An innocent person. You've never killed an innocent person before. We've always been so civilized about it. Who was it?"

"Hildegarde Kohner."

"Oh." Estella lit another cigarette and fanned the match out slowly, a puzzled look on her face. "Her?" She exhaled a long stream of smoke and then said, almost cheerily, "Well, that's not so bad. I never liked her. But a mistake is still a mistake, Achille. It was unspeakably careless of you."

"It might not have happened if we had followed my original idea to lock Natasha inside a freezer."

"Such a boring way to die."

"But it might have worked. And I could have finished off my dinner without indigestion."

"Well, then I guess it's back to the old *boring* board."

"Estella, you're ridiculing me."

She smiled and put her hand to her breast in mock amazement. "I? Ridicule you? No, darling, you must be thinking of a hundred other people."

"Estella, I've come here because I need your help."

"But you've always needed my help, Achille. From the very beginning. Well, what kind of help do you want now? Do you want more money to start another magazine? Do you want a loan to buy a freezer? Perhaps you'd like me to lose the weight for you? By the way, darling, you don't look any thinner to me. Have you really been dieting, or are you still glutting yourself like a Périgord goose?"

"I demand you stop this at once," he shouted. "Don't you realize that the police will be after me?"

"Why? You didn't mean to kill Hildegarde. It was an accident. However, you did make a serious mistake, Achille. You should have stayed there as we had planned. As though you were innocent. Instead, you've focused needless attention on yourself. But they have no evidence. There's nothing they can prove. I'm the one who bought you the false passports, the mixer, and the explosive. And as long as you're a good boy, all of Estella's horses and all of Estella's men will keep little Achille safe again."

He watched her as she walked from window to window correcting the way the drapes were hung. Estella was right. What could they prove? He could say he had run from Harrods because he was upset. That he wanted to see Estella. And that was the truth. But she thought he had made a mistake. Suppose she sought revenge and abandoned him?

"Estella, if you say anything to the police, ever, you will become an accessory to the murders. They will take you out of your robin's egg and put you into a small, dark, damp cell in which you will spend the rest of your life. The only mistakes you'll chart will be those of the rats who gnaw hungrily at your tattered clothes. The police will lock you up forever."

"They can't. It was you who made the mistake. It was your mistake, not mine. Give me back my list."

Achille handed it to her. She tore it into shreds and sat down at her desk. She took a fresh sheet of blue notepaper and dipped her pen into the ink. "Here," she said, holding out the freshly scratched note, "I've revised my instructions." He took the note and stared disbelievingly at the scrawled message.

He had lost Estella forever. The finality was overwhelming. The grief unbearable. He said for the last time, "Estella, I have always loved you."

"And I have endured you, Achille. I don't want to see you any more. You are repellent to me. You've allowed too many mistakes. Seven typographical errors in one issue. God knows how you managed to keep the murders quiet." She went to the file cabinet and unlocked it. She opened the second drawer. It, too, was empty except for a single sheet of blue notepaper. "My count is twelve photographers, twenty-eight proofreaders, six editors, fourteen printers, and the secretary who spilled tea on one of the galley sheets. How did you manage to kill them without a mistake?"

"Estella, for years I have been taking your little blue notes home with me. Kill the photographer. Kill the proofreader. Kill the editor. Kill the printer. Do you know, Estella, what I did with those little blue notes? I threw them away. I tossed them out. I dismissed your instructions. Listen to me carefully, Estella. I did not kill them."

"Well, then, who did?"

"No one did. They are all still very much alive. The twelve photographers, the twenty-eight proofreaders . . ."

Estella stepped back. She put her hand to her mouth and screamed. "You betrayed me! You told me they were dead."

He smiled. "They are alive, Estella. At this very moment, they are taking out-of-focus photographs, they are misspelling words, they are making mistake after mistake after mistake."

"Liar! You told me you had killed them. Achille, tell me they're dead!"

"Some of them are even hyphenating words incorrectly."

"Oh, my God. They're all still alive. Then the only one who was killed was the first one. The one I killed. You've lied to me all these years. You never killed anyone for me. You only killed for yourself. What kind of marriage is that?" She began tearing all of her blue notepaper into shreds.

"And, Estella, there's something else I haven't told you. Something you certainly should know. There were not one hundred and twelve errors. There were one hundred and thirteen. The one hundred and thirteenth was such an obvious one. How could you have missed it?"

"There were one hundred and twelve!" She began throwing the galley sheets at Achille. "You're trying to destroy me. But no matter how hard you try, I'm on to you now. I know they're alive. And I'll get them. I'll correct every last mistake."

A nurse ran into the room. "Mrs. van Golk, what is it?"

"Get him out of here. He's a liar. Get him out of here. It's Wednesday. He's made a mistake. He's not supposed to be here. It's Wednesday."

"Please, Mr. van Golk."

"They're all alive. He didn't kill them for me. They're all still out there. I've got to stop them. I've got to get out of here."

Two male attendants ran into the room and held Estella while the nurse injected her with a tranquilizer. Achille's eyes filled with tears. He crumpled the note on which Estella had written KILL YOURSELF and dropped it to the floor.

"Get him out of here," she shouted as he turned to leave. "It's not Thursday." Achille walked down the corridor. Frightened faces peered out from open doorways as Estella's screams were heard.

"Monsieur."

Achille had not seen the police approaching him. "What is it?"

"We must ask you to come with us at once. Scotland Yard has ordered your immediate return to London."

"Indeed." But there was no evidence, he thought. Estella was right, as always. There was no evidence. He had just destroyed the last of it.

NEW SCOTLAND YARD

Division of Homicide

From: Detective Inspector Carmody
To: Inspector Gilli Rome
       Inspector Griege Paris
       Inspector Friemond Geneva

Enclosed you will find the one hundred and sixty-three (163) documents and statements relating to the case of THE CROWN VS. ACHILLE VAN GOLK. I greatly appreciate your co-operation in permitting access to your files as well as for having obtained supplementary statements for us. I do not believe we would have been able to prepare charges against van Golk for the death of Hildegarde Kohner were it not for our ability to relate her death to a larger pattern.

Indeed this has been a most difficult case to assemble on all levels. Our only lead was Miss O'Brien's testimony that van Golk had told her the killer was an accountant named Arnold Tresting. (Tresting subsequently suffered a fatal heart attack while sleeping in the cinema.) Our only possible witness is the accused's wife, an incurable paranoid. As you will see from the documents enclosed, we have tried to avoid submitting her statements as evidence, although without them we could not have prepared any case whatsoever.

We have begun with the accused's medical report, in which his personal physician states that his life was threatened by his dietary habits. The statements of our psychiatrists each characterize van Golk as an extremely disturbed personality easily capable of acts of violence.

Our position was that the accused sought to avenge his declining physical condition by murdering the chefs whose food he valued most. We have the testimony of seven witnesses to a celebration prepared by Kohner, Fenegretti, Moulineaux, and O'Brien in response to the accused's request for his favorite dinner. The theory that the accused could have planned to kill each chef symbolically according to the dish each prepared, and in the sequence of the courses themselves, was upheld by statements from our psychiatrists, and from the accused's wife. We were advised that Mrs. van Golk's statements are not automatically to be discounted because of her mental condition, but that we would be ill advised to try to present such testimony to a jury.

We have been able to establish only the following:

DEATH OF LOUIS KOHNER

1. Van Golk has no witnesses to verify his alibi that he was at home asleep.
2. We do not have any witnesses who saw him at the scene of the crime.

DEATH OF NUTTI FENEGRETTI

1. Airline records show that van Golk flew from London to Geneva and back.
2. We have evidence that Mrs. van Golk secured a false Swiss passport, containing a picture of the accused, in the name of Hugo Victor. (We have not been able to find this passport and presume it has been destroyed.)
3. Dr. Enstein has confirmed he agreed to provide the accused with an alibi for that afternoon, but clearly the doctor did not know the accused's motivation. Although the accused flew to Geneva allegedly to see his wife, he did not see her that afternoon.
4. Airline records show a passenger named Hugo Victor traveled from Geneva to Rome and back within the time period the accused was allegedly in Geneva.
5. Estimated time of death of Fenegretti coincides with the time Hugo Victor was in Rome.

DEATH OF JEAN-CLAUDE MOULINEAUX

1. The accused has witnesses who saw him board a train to Brighton, and who saw him leave Victoria Station after allegedly returning from Brighton. There are no witnesses who actually saw him in Brighton.
2. We have evidence that Mrs. van Golk secured a false British passport, containing a picture of the accused, in the name of Hardy Thomas. (We have not been able to find this passport either.)
3. During the time the accused was allegedly in Brighton, airline records show that a passenger named Hardy Thomas traveled from London to Paris and back.
4. Estimated time of death of Moulineaux coincides with the time Hardy Thomas was in Paris.

DEATH OF HILDEGARDE KOHNER

1. We have evidence that Mrs. van Golk procured an electric mixer fitted with a detonating device, as well as an amount of plastic explosive known as C3.
2. We have statements that someone impersonating a female employee of the BBC arranged for and insisted upon the use of the mixer which contained the bomb.
3. Our psychiatrists concur that if the accused had been innocent, he would not have fled from Harrods in order to see his wife in Geneva.

We based our case on the fact that the accused was

in collusion with his wife, taking full advantage of her distressed mental state. We argued it was the intent of the accused to murder Natasha O'Brien and that Mrs. Kohner was killed due to her unexpected use of the mixer.

Needless to say, we would not have been able to construct the plot this far were it not for your mutual co-operation. It is with regret, therefore, that I report to you the final disposition of this case.

We were prepared that a case predicated so heavily upon psychiatric supposition, and supported only by the testimony of the accused's insane wife, might well be dismissed before being brought to trial. However, we were not prepared for the suggestion from sources close to 10 Downing Street (who assured us the matter had NOT been discussed with the Royal Family) that we negotiate with the defendant and accept his solicitor's compromise that we refrain from pressing charges if the accused would admit himself to an institution for psychiatric care. (It appears that Mrs. van Golk is related to the Foreign Secretary, and the accused has himself been a frequent visitor to Buckingham Palace.) I was assured that if we had a stronger case, under no circumstances would there have been any suggestion of compromise.

Achille van Golk is presently a patient at St. Anthony's Clinic, where we have him under surveillance until his departure within a few days to the Enstein Clinic in Geneva.

Although it was decided, against my judgment, to close this case, I realize you are not bound by considerations which determined the disposition in London. While I cannot, in an official capacity, provoke any further local investigation, I most certainly would be bound to honor any such requests you might have while preparing your own cases which I presume you are developing with utmost dispatch. Surely, any co-operation on my part with your own local investigations is merely reciprocating the courtesy shown to me, and cannot be viewed as contrary to policy.

Of course, it is obvious that in a sense our investigation in London has precluded any effective conclusion to this case. We have been advised by van Golk's solicitors that if any charges are pressed, at any time, the plea would be innocence by reason of insanity.

he band was playing *Keep Your Sunny Side Up!* American Good Foods had rented the ballroom at the Dorchester in London for its press party announcing the opening of the H. Dumpty chain. The room was filled with reporters, cameramen, food editors, restaurant people, executives, and the customary "fillers" who made a gathering into a crowd. Four chefs stood in a circle in the center of the room and made omelettes. Waiters dressed as Humpty Dumpty carried large trays laden with glasses of champagne. Huge baskets were filled with yellow and white sunflowers, daisies, and chrysanthemums.

"Is it true, Mr. Ogden, that your firm has funded a study to disprove the dangers of egg cholesterol?"

"Well, how many chickens have coronaries?" Max smiled and drank some of the ginger ale that was in his champagne glass.

"And what about your chefs? Mr. Ogden, are they all imported from France?"

"Just our head chef, Auguste. All the others will be trained by him."

"Someone said you had tried to hire each of the chefs who were killed recently."

"Why don't we forget about that. It's last month's news."

"How will H. Dumpty be different from the other omelette restaurants in London? Why do you think we need another fast-food outlet?"

"Fast food is only for people who are fasting. We're different. We're using only fresh ingredients. Nothing in a tin can, nothing frozen, nothing packaged."

"Isn't that rather un-American of you?"

"Good business is never un-American."

"How about a picture of you making an omelette?"

"I thought you'd never ask." Max began walking through the crowd, smiling, saying his excuse me's as he nodded hello to people he had never before seen. Word spread among the photographers that he would be making an omelette and they began converging upon the circle of chefs. Max walked over to Auguste. "I'll give you a dollar later," he whispered. "I want to make one."

"You will ruin everything," Auguste hissed angrily.

"Two dollars."

Auguste shrugged his shoulders and stepped aside. "Okay, gang. Here's how you do it. Take two eggs from Mother Nature's specially designed 'crack pack,' tickle them with a steel fork, and add a teaspoon of water. Use a seasoned pan that's been doing nothing but omelettes. Add butter—not margarine—and get it really hot. Let the butter bubble and then, before it turns brown, add the eggs. Scratch their backs with the fork a few times and start folding. No omelette should take longer to make than thirty seconds. Fold it out onto a plate and *voilà!* Who's daring enough to taste it?"

"I am."

Max turned quickly. It was Natasha. She smiled at him and extended her arm to take the plate. He stared back, smiling broadly. Natasha wore a metallic-silver-and-brown zebra-striped pants suit. Her beige satin blouse matched the turban on her head. Without taking her eyes from him, she cut into the center of the omelette.

"Aren't you going to taste it, Miss O'Brien?" a reporter asked.

"Where have you been since the murders, Miss O'Brien?"

"Are you two planning to get married again?"

Max walked around the table and took Natasha's hand. They made their way through the crowd, out of the ballroom, and closed the door behind them. Max took her in his arms and they kissed, holding each other tightly. Then Natasha slowly rubbed her cheek against his.

Max sniffed and cleared his throat. "Well, you sure screwed up my press party." They kissed again, but were jostled apart by someone trying to open the door. "Let's find someplace we can be alone." He took her hand and began walking down the carpeted hallway looking for a door, for a place to be alone. He brought her fingers to his lips and kissed them. With his other hand, he opened the first door he found.

"I may be drunk," announced a small woman in an enormous flowered hat, "but I'd recognize the two of you anywhere. I'm the bride's aunt." The room was filled with hundreds of people, and the band was playing *Sunrise, Sunset.* Natasha and Max looked at one another and started to laugh.

"It's my hat, isn't it?" the woman said, drinking a glass of champagne. "Well, I don't care."

"So, what are you doing without a little food? Look how skinny you keep her. Over here." A large man with a cigar in his mouth grabbed Max by the arm and led them to the buffet table.

"I'm so pleased you could come," a passing woman in a purple gown said to Natasha. "You're looking so well."

"Millie, what are we doing here?"

"Being alone," he said, kissing her on the cheek. "They'll never find us here." He took two plates and handed one to her. He dug a spoon into a chopped liver swan that wore a gold crown inscribed *Good Luck, Brenda and Bernie.* "We never had a swan," he said. "Maybe when I grow up . . ."

"Millie, we are grown up."

"Did we grow up good?"

"I think so."

"Have some cole slaw," he said, heaping her plate. "What are we going to be now that we're grown up?"

"Together."

"Like Brenda and Bernie?"

"No." She turned from him. "Have some meatballs."

"Then like who?" he asked as they continued walking around the buffet.

"Like you and me."

"You mean together, but not Together."

"I'm just not ready for a chopped liver swan. But I love you, Millie, and I want to be with you."

"Why did you run away? You should have seen me the day I came to the hospital to get you. I'd rented a carriage with two white horses. And then they gave me your letter. 'I need time. Be patient. I'll be back.' It was like a mash note from General MacArthur."

"I needed the time, Millie." She spooned some herring over his meatballs. "To collect myself and try to put the pieces back. I missed you so. I had to stop myself from phoning."

"Where the hell were you?" He began piling her plate with sardines, as the band played *If I Were a Rich Man.*

"I went to Vienna. It was the only place I could feel close to Hildegarde. I went back to look at the house we lived in. I walked down familiar streets remembering things she had said. I did a lot of crying."

"A whole month of crying?"

"No," she said, putting some turkey slices over his herring. "I went back to New York. I sat home mostly. As much as I tried, I couldn't get myself to hate Achille. Even knowing that he meant to kill me too."

"Well, if you're here to start the Achille van Golk fan club . . ."

"You know what I mean. There was so much more sadness than anger. Oh, Millie, there was such a great sadness."

"As sad as what's on your plate?" he asked. They looked at the dishes, piled high with herring mixed into meatballs and dozens of sardines pressed into chopped liver. He put his arms around her.

"I've been offered a job as editor of LUCULLUS," she said.

"I heard."

"I'm taking it."

"I heard that too."

"What haven't you heard?"

He raised his eyebrows. "I haven't heard *why*."

She leaned her head on his shoulder as they danced. "To be near you."

"Yeah? But not as near as . . ."

"Brenda and Bernie? No."

"Isn't London or LUCULLUS the last place you'd want to be?"

"I don't want any ghosts, Millie. I have to come back here to get rid of them. Otherwise I'll carry them around always."

"Yes, General."

"Millie . . ."

"Yeah?"

"You haven't said you loved me."

He kissed her on the mouth. He kissed her on the

nose. He kissed her on the eyes. Then he kissed her ear and whispered, "So fuck the swan!"

Achille lay on the bed in his locked room at St. Anthony's Clinic. It had been an exhausting day. But the long month of waiting would end tomorrow when he left for Geneva.

The designs for his suite at the Enstein Clinic were finally finished to his specifications. The suite would duplicate exactly his flat on Hertford Street. He had even completed the arrangements for Cesar to travel first class with him in the morning. He was most upset about the decision not to transport his wine cellar, but clearly the wine would not travel well and those bottles that did would take years to regain their composure. The sale of his cellar would bring him more than enough to duplicate most of it from local merchants in Geneva.

However, apprehension that the French or Italian police would reopen the case nagged at him. If they were to pursue it, and if somehow they found a witness who could testify to his presence in either Paris or Rome on the days in question, he would have to plead insanity and have the courts negotiate his being institutionalized. But, his solicitors explained, the longer the police took in commencing their investigations, the less likely they would be to find anyone who remembered seeing him. The thought that he could not release himself at will was intolerable.

And there was still the problem of Estella. Enstein assured him that she would not recall his last visit unless there was an improvement in her condition. In which case, not only would she remember the visit, but her testimony could be accepted in any court. The immediate project, then, was to ensure that Estella did not recover, and that their weekly luncheons continued. Enstein had agreed for medical reasons it would be best not to tell Estella that Achille was himself living in another wing.

He knew he would not miss London. At least not for a while. Surely the clinic was the best place for him to be while he was on his diet. But after that? Who knows?'

There was a knock at the door.

"There is no one here," he called.

"Dinner, sir," the nurse replied.

"Ah, yes, time for victuals at the Château d'If." He heard the key in the lock and then watched as Sister Angelica wheeled in a large cart. "And what have the saints preserved for me tonight?" he said, raising himself to a sitting position.

"It's a surprise, Mr. van Golk. Some gentlemen were here from a food club, the friends of good food, I believe?"

"Les Amis de Cuisine?"

"Yes, that's it. I knew it was an Italian name. They came by in a truck and said that they knew you were leaving in the morning and they wanted to express the esteem in which they hold you by bringing you a special dinner."

"A belated attempt to curry my good favor," Achille said.

"Well, I know they had to get special permission. And they made me promise not to peek until I brought it in here."

296

"Well, let's see what those ingrates have sent. Ah, Lafite '45."

"The gentlemen said they had already taken out the cork so that it would have . . . sneezed?"

"Breathed. Wine breathes. Now please leave. I find your clothes very depressing."

"But I'm supposed to serve you dinner."

"Better to serve the Lord. He's less demanding. I wish to be alone."

"But Mr. van Golk, the rules explicitly require . . ."

"I make the rules within this domain. And I choose to dine alone. Get out!"

"I shall report this at once." She turned and left. He heard the key in the door, locking him in.

As if greeting an old friend, Achille stood up and put his hand to the Lafite. The temperature was perfect. Such a noble companion for dinner. He picked up the crystal wine glass and gently began pouring. His mind flashed to the Château. Laughing with the Baron in the Salon Rouge as they drank his last bottle of the 1869 vintage.

Achille held his glass to the light. He stood tall, greeting the authority and breeding in his goblet. Smiling, he swirled the wine and lifted the glass to his nose. Violets. Raspberries. He sipped. He sighed. Superb.

He leaned over and lifted the cover from the Georgian silver platter. When he saw what was there, artfully arranged on trimmed toast, elegantly garnished with sprigs of parsley, Achille dropped the cover to the floor.

He shuddered and then began to cry

URDER...
AYHEM...
YSTERY...

From Ballantine

KEEPING YOU ON THE EDGE OF YOUR SEAT...

Spellbinding suspense from Ballantine Books